DEDICATION

To my wife Karen, and four boys – Dylan, Brad, Ky, and Makenzie.

CONTENTS

CHAPTER 1

The Alleyway

Bang, and the heat from my right leg and the pain made me realise that I had just been kneecapped.

"Fenian lover!" one of the men shouted at me.

Bang, and my left leg done. The pain was now so severe I screamed out, "Fuck, fuck, fuck! Stop! Please stop!"

"You deserve it, Fenian lover. This is your fault for knowing this I.R.A. bastard."

Then I knew Gerrerd was lying next to me. He started screaming, "No, don't! Don't!"

His cries were drowning out my tears and screams as I heard one of them shout, "Do him! Do him now!"

Bang, and the screams from Gerrerd stopped.

"You are a lucky man, Jonny," one of them shouted as I heard a car door slam and a car screech its tyres as it sped away.

As I lay there in the alleyway just off the Shankill road, I felt so cold and tired. The pain had all but gone but I felt blood ooze out of both my legs and my jeans were soaked. I reached down to feel my legs, not sure if it was blood or piss, but I knew I was in trouble as I couldn't feel my feet and couldn't move my legs. My thoughts turned to Gerrerd as I pulled off the bag that was over my head. I was horrified to see Gerrerd lying beside me with half his face missing. I screamed, "Help me! Somebody fucking help me!" but I knew it would fall on deaf ears. My heart was racing and the more I panicked the more blood seemed to ooze out of my legs.

I lay back down and felt so cold and tired. I could hear my heart thump. *Bump, bump, bump, bump*. I was so tired and closed my eyes, waiting for help.

As I lay there, soaked with Gerrerd's and my own blood, I began to recall my life as a boy.

CHAPTER 2

My Saturday Job

It was 1991. I was fourteen years old, living in Broom Street just off the Shankill road. I was an only child living with my mum and dad, Annie and Jimmy. We were just a typical family, just struggling through life and all its difficulties, and this is my story.

Saturday morning, 5th November 1991, 07.30; my mum Annie came in and shook me.

"Jonny, Jonny! It's time to get up, you're going to be late for work."

I opened my eyes to my mum, who was standing over me dressed in her usual nightdress, with black hair and heavy build. She said again, "Come on, you lazy bones. Don't be keeping Nigel waiting."

Nigel was our lemonade man; I had been working as a Saturday boy for a few weeks now and really loved the job. It got me out of the house, away from my dad Jimmy, who was constantly shouting at me for just about anything. Also the money was good and Nigel always bought chips for lunch – that was a real treat as in our house there was barely a slice of bread, never mind chips out of the chippy.

I threw on my ripped jeans, an aul jumper that had seen better days, my socks and sizzler trainers, slapped some water round my face, flattened my sticking-up hair, brushed my teeth, had a piss, and I was set.

Down the stairs I went, to be met by my mum at the bottom who had a round of bread and jam and a hug.

"Have a nice day, son, and be careful."

Out the door I went, to be met with the bucketing rain.

"Bollocks," I said. "Another friggin' soak'n."

I horsed my jam butty into me before it went soggy and took to my heels down the Shankill road to meet Nigel in Dover Street for 8.15.

As I ran down past Shankill Leisure Centre, I heard a familiar voice. "Jonny, where you going?"

I stopped and turned. As it was pishing out of the heavens, my sizzlers couldn't take the sudden halt, and on my arse I went, smacking my elbows off the pavement.

"Fuck!" I shouted.

And standing over me was my mate Billy.

"You alright, Jonny?"

"Am I fuck," I said. "I think I've broke my fuckin' arm." Billy helped me up.

Billy lived not far from me and we went to the boys' model together. He was better off than me, lived in a big, fancy, three-bedroom house in Tennent Street with a garden, and his dad wasn't an alco and had a job.

I stood there, soaked to the skin, feeling sorry for myself, but wouldn't shed a tear; couldn't show I was in pain in front of Billy, he would have told the whole school.

"Where you going?" Billy asked again.

"I'm going to work, mate," I said as I rubbed my elbow, feeling for blood.

"Work? Where'd you get a job from?"

"I work for Nigel, the lemonade man," I replied.

"Lucky bastard," Billy said. "Can you get me a job?" he asked.

"I will ask him for you," I replied.

No chance, I thought. Billy would steal the eye out your head and if Nigel caught you thieving, out you go, and I would be ditched too.

"Here mate, you are soaked. Where is your coat?" Billy asked.

I didn't have a coat. The last one I had I used as a goal post up the Woodvale and when our team beat the Glencairn casuals, a row broke out and my coat got nicked, but that's another story.

"I forgot it, Billy. Bloody stupid of me a day like this," I replied.

"Here mate, take mine, I'm going home now anyway. I will call later and get it off you. What time you finished?"

"About half one, mate."

"Spot on, see you later." And Billy walked off.

Brilliant, a coat with a fucking hood. Happy as a pig in shit.

Off I limped, zipping the coat up to my chin as I walked past Kentucky to meet Nigel.

Into Dover Street and there was Nigel sitting parked in his big red Ford lorry. I thought to myself, *Hope he's got the heating on,* as I was Baltic, couldn't feel my now soaked feet or my hands. Holy fuck, they were sore with the cold, never mind my throbbing elbow. *Fuck Billy*, I thought. *Calling me, but then he did lend me his coat.*

As I opened up the passenger door of the lorry, I said, "What about you, Nigel? That's a quare morning to be selling lemonade."

"Alright son," Nigel replied. "We will get them all in a day like that, only us lemonade men and head cases out a morning like that."

Nigel always had an answer for you that would make you laugh.

"A new coat, I see. Think I'm paying you too much," he said.

"Dead on, Nigel. Speaking of money, I could do with a pay rise," I joked.

"We will see at the end of the day," Nigel replied.

Fuck, I was only joking, but chuffed at the thought of an extra couple of quid.

Off we went to start the run.

The first house I had to call on was wee Lily. She always took the same order – six cream sodas – and she always had a packet of crisps and a biscuit waiting for me. But more important was my 50p tip, and that's why being a lemonade man's helper was a great job – you always got as much in tips as you did wages. But I couldn't tell my da that, as he would have strapped them off me for a carry out and I would never have seen them again.

All bloody day that rain didn't stop. By 12 o'clock I was absolutely soaked to the knickers. Nigel was as well, but the work had to be done.

When we got to Conway Street Nigel always stopped for half an hour for lunch, and this was what I couldn't wait for – chips from the chippy! Loads of salt and vinegar and by God they were the nicest chips in the world. I ate them that quick my stomach thought my throat was cut.

"Slow down, Jonny. You need to come up for air," Nigel said.

I just looked over, my mouth full of chips, and smiled, swallowed what was in my mouth, and said, "Ano, Nigel. I was starving and the chips are great – thanks."

"Take a bottle of juice to wash them down, son," he said.

Out the door I went, and a big bottle of iron brew had my name on it.

Gulp, gulp, gulp, and I washed the chips down, gave a big burp, and that was me set to finish the run.

About another hour's work and our last call was

my house, and more important – wages time. I thought to myself as Nigel went into his pocket to get some money, *Is he going to give me an extra couple of quid?* The few seconds I waited felt like forever.

"There you go, Jonny. Your normal fiver and two quid extra for working so hard today."

Holy fuck, with tips and all I had fifteen quid – I was rolling in it. Never even crossed my mind that I was freezing and soaked, and the pain in my elbow was no more.

Nigel always threw in four bottles of lemonade for my house as well, so when I said to Nigel, "Thanks, see you next Saturday," I slammed the door shut and off Nigel drove.

In through the front door and there was my da lying on the sofa, and the room filled with smoke as he puffed his brains out watching the horse racing on the TV.

"Hi Da, how's it going?" I said.

He turned and looked at me. "Could be better if you could sponsor me a few quid for a beer," he asked.

"Tips weren't good today, not many people in," I replied, lying through my front teeth.

"Auk well, maybe better next week," he replied.

He bought it, thank fuck.

Out of the kitchen, my mum Annie came.

"Jesus Jonny, you're soaked. Away up and get them wet clothes off you before you catch your death."

"Mum, Mum," I said. "Nigel gave me a pay rise."

She looked at me and smiled. "You're well worth it, son. You're a great wee worker, Nigel is lucky to have you."

My mum always made me feel good about myself and as I walked up the stairs I was beaming from ear to ear, well chuffed at myself.

CHAPTER 3

A Smack Round The Head

It wasn't too long before a knock came to the front door, and my mum shouted up the stairs, "Jonny, Billy is at the door!"

I clambered down the stairs to see Billy at the front door.

"Alright Billy," I said. "What's the crack?"

"Apart from the one in your elbow," he replied, laughing, "nothing, mate."

I had all but forgot about my sore elbow and out the door I went, shouting behind me, "What time's tea, Ma?"

My mum replied, "Be back for six, Jonny."

Me and Billy walked up Broom Street, heading for the Woodvale park. The rain was starting to go off now and Billy said to me, "Well, did you ask Nigel for me for a job mate?"

Again lying through teeth, I replied, "Yes mate, but no luck. He only wants one helper."

"Fucker," Billy replied. "Could of done with a few quid a week."

I knew what Billy meant when he said a few quid. He would have robbed Nigel blind and any aul doll on the run as well. He really was a tea leaf, but he was my best mate.

Walking into the Woodvale park, we saw a lot of the boys from our school playing a match, and that was our passion – football, the beautiful game. I dreamt many a night of playing for my beloved Linfield.

"Yo Jonny, you're in our team!" shouted Stevo. "Billy, you can play for Davo's team."

Billy wasn't too well pleased, 'cause when he looked at Davo's team they were half of the Glencairn ones. My team was all the lads from the lower Shankill; hard as fuck, they were.

I played right wing and Billy played left back, so I had loads of chances to skin him, and skin him I did. When we played football we forgot about everything in our lives – it was on hold until Saturday afternoon up at the park and the match.

I received the ball from Stevo, the midfield enforcer, and one touch and I was away down the right wing; beat one, beat two, laughed as I skipped past Billy, and crossed the ball onto Bimbo's head. Gift of a goal, 1-0. Half the team ran over to me to celebrate. I would have been the youngest and skinniest player there, but loved the game and wouldn't back out of a tackle.

We won 4-1, and I got a goal into the bargain. Mucked up to the eyeballs but what a match and what a day.

I said my goodbyes to Billy. "See ya the mara mate."

"I'm going to my granny's the mara mate, so I will see you on the bus on Monday," replied Billy.

"No worries Billy, see you then."

And off I walked down home.

I walked through the front door and snuck straight up the stairs, trying to avoid my ma and da. They would have cracked if they had seen the state of my jeans and trainers. I stripped off and threw my clothes into the aul wicker basket in the bathroom. I started washing my trainers in the sink when the smell of aul stale smoke hit me, and I knew my da was standing behind me. My heart missed a beat.

"Look at the state of you!"

And a clip round the back of the head I got.

"You're fucking stinking. Do you think your ma hasn't anything better to do than wash your clothes?"

Another smack round the head. This time my da caught me right – my ear was throbbing.

"Da! Da, stop. I was playing a match."

Fighting back the tears, I heard my mum come up the stairs.

"Jimmy, Jimmy! Stop, leave him alone. He's only a child."

"Old enough for a good dig, and I'm the man to do it."

"Jimmy, here, are you not meeting your mates for a pint?" my mum asked.

Straight away my da stopped and turned to face my mum. She had a tenner in her hand and my da said, "Spot on, love," and snatched the tenner out of her hand. He pushed past her and shouted behind him as he slammed the front door shut, "I'll be home when I'm home."

My da always drank in the Moutain View club not far from our house, and it was always the same outcome – only came home when he ran out of money.

Thank fuck, I thought to myself as I rubbed my right ear.

"You alright, son?" my mum asked.

"Yeah Mum, just glad he's away out."

"So am I, love. So am I."

Standing there in just my boxers, I felt a bit embarrassed with my mum standing looking at me. I sort of tried to cover myself, and there was that split moment, I think me and my mum were a bit scundered.

"Come 'ere you, and give your ma a hug. You're not too aul for that."

My mum was a lovely person and I loved her to bits. A big hug and everything was fine.

"Get yourself washed, your tea's on the table." And off she went down the stairs.

I finished off washing my trainers and then refilled the sink and got a quick wash – and it was a quick wash, the water was bloody freezing.

I threw on a pair of jammies and went down for my tea.

As I sat at our table in the living room to sausages, beans, and spuds (my favourite dinner), I noticed my mum sitting over in the corner rubbing her eyes.

"You tired, Mum?" I asked as I looked up at the clock. It read 6.30.

"No," she replied, "just got something in my eye."

I stopped eating and walked over. "What's wrong, Ma?" I asked.

"That was my last tenner, love, but don't worry."

How could you not? *My da's a bastard,* I thought.

"It will be alright Mum, something will turn up."

"Aye love, I hope so," she replied. "Away and finish your tea."

Every mouthful, I could hardly swallow at the thought of my da sitting round there in the pub, laughing and joking with his alco mates, and my ma sitting here skint and all the worries in the world.

I finished my tea and put the plate in the sink, and went upstairs into my room.

I reached under my bed. Hidden away in the corner under a spare blanket was my tin – I kept my money in it. Over the weeks working for Nigel I always took a couple of quid out and put it in there. Every time I opened it I prayed my da hadn't found it and emptied it. It rattled – good sign my da hadn't got it. I opened the lid and emptied the money onto my bed. Twenty-eight quid should be there, and yep, every pound accounted for. I counted out twenty and set it aside, put the other eight quid back in and hid it back under my bed. I lifted the money and walked back downstairs, then went over to where my mum was slouched in her chair with her head in her hands.

"Mum," I said quietly.

She looked up.

"What, Jonny?" she asked.

I opened my hands. "Here," I said. "Will this do you?"

Her eyes lit up. "Jonny, where'd you get all that money?"

"Working for Nigel. I put some away every week," I replied.

"No, Jonny. I can't take it, you worked too hard for it."

"I don't need it, Mum. You take it, I will save it up again, but don't tell my da."

"Jonny, you're a wee angel – a life saver."

As I poured the money into my Mum's opened hands, I felt fantastic and just wanted her to be happy, even just for a split second.

She gave me a big hug and said, "Don't be saying anything to your da, and Jonny, don't hide your money all in the one place. If your da finds it he will take it off you and either drink it or give it to the bookies."

"Yeah Ma, you're right. I'll do that."

I lay down on the sofa. The fire was lit and the Dukes of Hazzard was coming on; life was good, I thought.

"Jonny, are you alright here for an hour?"

"Yeah Ma, why?" I asked.

"I was to meet June for the bingo, but I'll not go if you don't want me to."

"No, it's fine Ma. Go, you never go out, but don't home come if you don't win." I laughed.

She kissed me on the head and said, "I will get Martha next door to keep an eye on you."

"No worries, Ma. I'll be fine."

And out the door she went.

Happy days; house to myself and most important, I had the remote for the TV.

I started watching Dukes of Hazzard and with the heat of the fire, I was out like a light, snoring my head off, dreaming of playing for Linfield someday.

God knows how long I was sleeping but I woke with a jerk as the front door opened. My first thought was, *Hope it's my ma and not my drunken da.* I looked up and it was my ma, and she had chips with her. Happy days.

"Get the teapot on, Jonny. I have something to tell you."

"What, Ma? What is it?"

"Remember you said don't come home unless I won? Well I did, Jonny. I did!"

She was so excited; she opened her purse and it was full of notes.

"Fuck me, Ma. Oops. Sorry Ma. Sorry for cursing."

"You're alright, son," she replied as she lifted a fist

full of notes out of her purse.

I had never seen so much money. "How much, Ma? How much?"

"150 quid. The jackpot, Jonny – the bloody jackpot."

"Oh my god, Ma. We're rich! We're rich!"

She reached into the money and lifted twenty quid out. "That's for you, son. Go and hide it away and don't tell your da about it."

"I won't, Ma."

I took the stairs two at a time up to my room, and reached under my bed for the tin. Just as I opened the lid I remembered what my ma had told me, so I put the lid back on and back under the bed with it.

As I stood there wondering where to hide the money, I looked up at the wall where my Man U picture was that my mum had got me for Christmas last year. Yep, that was where my money was going. I lifted it off the wall and turned it round, opened up the back a bit, and slipped the twenty quid in it, then put it back up on the wall and fixed it straight. I touched the front and said, "Big Norm, you look after that for me."

Norman Whiteside played for Man U. He was my hero. He grew up on the Shankill just like me, and I thought if he could make it so could I.

"Jonny, here's your supper," I heard my mum call from downstairs.

I went downstairs; it was about 10.30 now and the smell of chips was making my mouth water. There, sat at the table was my mum, a big mug of tea, and a couple rounds of Ohara's big bread with loads of butter. Life was good.

As we tucked into the chips, in through the front door my da fell. *Aah fuck*, I thought. My mum got up straight away and said, "Get up, Jimmy, you're drunk. Come on, I'll help you up the stairs."

My da staggered to his feet. "I'm alright. Get the teapot on, Annie. I could murder a sandwich."

Just at that, he looked over at me. "What you got there, Jonny?"

"Chips, Da."

"Happy days," he said, and staggered over. Lifting a handful from the vinegar-soaked paper, he opened his mouth and in the chips went.

I looked at what was left and thought, *They aren't gonna last long*, and lifted a handful myself, put them between a round of bread, and scarpered up to my room.

I knew if I had stayed downstairs my chip butty would have been gone as well.

I finished my supper and got into bed, hoping my da would fall asleep on the sofa as usual.

CHAPTER 4

The Fight With The Spider

The next morning, I woke. Sunday. Great, no school, but as per usual a trip down to my nan's, who lived just off Tennent Street in Orkney Street.

But there was the matter of breakfast, and to see what form my da was in first.

Down the stairs I went. My mum was already up and tidying the house. "Would you like a bowl of cornflakes Jonny?" she asked.

"Yeah Ma, that would be great."

"You will need to nip to the shop for milk, son," she asked.

I threw on my trainers, which were lying by the fire. They had now dried out after I had washed them, and my mum gave me a quid and out the door I went.

The shop was just on our corner, and two minutes ran me up and down again. It was bloody freezing as I ran down the street in my jammies.

As I came back in the front door my da was coming down the stairs; he was still wearing the same clothes as he had gone to the bar in last night, and a big feg in his gob. He looked rough – a dirty aul unshaven face and his aul slippers that had seen better days.

"Alright Jonny," he said.

"Alright Da," I replied as I walked into the kitchen and handed my ma the milk and her change.

"Thanks Jonny." She whispered, "Mum's the word," and she winked at me.

I knew what she meant – tell my da nothing about the bingo.

A big bowl of cornflakes and loads of sugar – beaut!

I sat down at the table and my da was already there, smoking his brains out as usual. I horsed the cornflakes into me as quick as I could, and every other mouthful I might as well have been smoking myself, as I breathed in my da's aul smoke.

Me and my da never really got on. I hated his drinking and the way he treated my ma so we never really got into any conversation, so it was a case of hello and goodbye. I just tried to stay out of his way.

I went up the stairs and got washed and changed; the morning just went as usual – my da on the sofa and my ma cleaning the house.

It was about 2.30 when my mum said, "Right boys, let's go and see your nanny."

My da replied, "Yous go ahead, I will come down shortly."

Same old crap. My da never went, he and my nanny never got on. He would be in the same spot when we returned.

I loved it when it was just me and my mum; she always asked how my week went as we walked down to my nanny's. I would tell her about the match – she always looked like she enjoyed me telling her about skinning players and scoring goals.

To be honest she probably couldn't care less, but she made me feel like she did.

When we got to my nanny's the rain was just starting to come on, so good timing.

My nanny was a wee woman; jet black hair but had a really fierce temper – she always said it as it was, and that's why my da wouldn't come down. I remember one time when she tore strips off him about his drinking and told him to go and get a job. I was about ten years old but remember it clearly as he answered her back. He told her to shut her bloody mouth and mind her own fuck'n business.

What a mistake that was. She lifted the poker from the fire and beat him two or three times with it. As he ran out the front door she swung again at him, narrowly missing his head. She hit the door frame and she shouted after him, "Don't show your face round here again, you lazy bugger!"

As I walked into the house I looked up, and the big chunk out of the door frame was still there. I think she left it there to remind my da if he ever decided to visit.

I smiled to myself and thought, *I would never speak back to her like that.*

"Hiya Nanny," I said as I walked over and hugged her.

"How are you, Jonny?" she replied.

"All good, Nanny."

"Hi Mum, how are you today?" my mum asked.

"Aright love, how are you?"

"Ok Mum. Close your eyes?" she asked.

"What for, love?"

"Just close your eyes. I have something for you."

My nanny closed her eyes and my mum put two twenty pound notes into her hands.

She immediately opened her eyes. "Oh my god, love. What are you doing? Where'd you get the money from?"

My mum said, "I won the bingo last night, Mum. The jackpot – 150 quid."

"Oh my goodness, that's fantastic, but I can't take this. You keep it."

"No Mum, I want you to have it. You're always giving me money."

"Ok love, thanks very much."

My nanny was as skint as us but always seemed to help us out when my da had done the money in, so I think my mum took great joy when she was able to give her some money back. She seemed to be glowing as I looked at her.

My granda had passed away years ago; I never really knew him as I was a baby, but my mum always told me stories about him working in the shipyard over in East Belfast, and how he walked to and from work six days a week. He was an ex-soldier who fought in the Second World War, and a well-respected man. I sometimes wish that I had known him 'cause I would have loved to hear his stories about the war and how many Germans he killed. My nanny never mentioned him, I think it brought back too many memories and how she missed him. It was probably easier for her not to talk about him.

"Jonny, away in and put the teapot on, son," my nanny asked as she gave my mum a hug.

My nanny always made the same sandwich – the ham out of the tin – and I always seemed to get the bit with all the bloody jelly still on it. As I sat there in front of the fire picking the jelly off the ham, my nanny said, "Eat it up, Jonny. That's the best bit, it will put hair on your chest."

Yeah right, I thought, and I snickered at the thought of me getting changed for P.E. in school and having this big hairy chest. What would my mates say?

"What you laughin' at, Jonny?" she asked.

"Nothing Nanny," I said, as I ate my nice jelly ham sandwich, washing it down with a gulp of tea.

I finished my lunch and set my cup and plate into the sink. "Nanny, is it alright if I use your toilet?" I asked.

"Of course, love. You don't need to ask."

Out the back door and into my nanny's wee small

yard; the only things in it were the coal hole and the toilet, and with it being November it was going to be a cold seat.

As I pulled open the wooden door that was falling apart, I reached around the corner, feeling for the string to pull the light on, and probably should have left the light off. The bloody spiders were everywhere. I lifted the newspaper that was on the ground and had the fight of my life. I swear one of those spiders turned and growled at me; I must have hit it two or three times and the bloody thing never flinched. I threw the newspaper towards the ceiling to try and kill it but missed and hit the board that was the ceiling. It fell to the floor and something fell down with it and smacked me on the head, knocking me to the ground. When I got to my feet I looked towards the house hoping my mum and nanny hadn't heard anything. Nope, I was fine. I felt my head for blood, and I felt a big bump. *Fuck, that was sore*, I thought to myself. I sneezed with the dust and rubbed my eyes.

As I looked to the floor I saw a rusty aul tin and I lifted it – it was an old biscuit tin that had been sealed with sellotape. I set it on the toilet seat so I could lift the board and put it back up, so if my mum or nanny came out they wouldn't shout. I closed the door behind me and sat on the toilet to open the tin; inside was a gun. I lifted it to look at it, it was really heavy and was stinking. It looked like a gun a cowboy would have used and as I examined it further I noticed it was loaded – it had seven bullets in it and it scared the crap out of me. I had never seen a gun before, never mind held one.

I set it down to see what else was in the box.

There were some old photos and a folded up piece of paper with names and addresses written on it. As I looked at the photos, one of them was of a man and woman who looked like they were about twenty or so. I turned it round and it said 'Lilly and Jim 1939'. I looked at it again; oh my god, that was my nanny and the man was my granda, and it hit me – the gun must have been my granda's.

I heard the back door open.

"Jonny, you finished yet? We are heading home now," my mum said.

"Just a minute Mum, coming now."

I put the gun and photos back in the tin, put the lid on it, and stood up on the toilet. I moved the board over slightly and hid the tin, then I replaced the board and flushed the toilet.

I thought to myself, *No way am I going for a crap in there. I will nip it till I get home,* and slammed the door shut.

We left my nanny's after a while and headed back up home.

By the time I got home it was a quick dash up the stairs and onto the toilet – I just made it.

CHAPTER 5

A Face Full Of Custard

Monday came round too quick, as I was out the door and met Billy at the bus stop to get the bus for school. Billy was a couple of years older than me so he was in fifth year; I was in third year but we were good mates and had been friends for a while now.

As we got on the bus it was bunged as usual, standing room only, and the journey took about ten minutes to the boys' model on the Ballysillan road.

My reg class was Mr Walkingshaw, a tough, well-built man who had a glass eye and a temper you wouldn't mess with.

I remember one day in class we were all messing around and Walkingshaw wasn't going to put up with it; he ordered three of the toughest boys in our year out of class for messing and as we all tried to see what was going on through the frosted glass, aul Billy was fair digging the three of them. It lasted about two minutes and when the four of them came back into class you could have heard a pin drop. Jonty, Paul, and Jason all came in holding their jaws, and Billy said, "Right class, back to work."

Holy fuck, I thought. *He's just knocked the melt out of the three of them.* After that day nobody messed around again, and when you saw Billy anywhere, you kept your head down and just faded into the background.

After reg I had double maths; I loved this subject. I think working with Nigel on Saturdays and working with money gave me a different way of counting, and I found problem solving easy.

Lunch time was great, and a race to the lunch hall was a must. The quicker you got there the more chance you had for seconds.

In the queue for lunch it was the usual suspects, Jonty at the front followed by his two henchmen, Paul and Jason. I got in about tenth so the chances were good for seconds.

The closer I got to the top of the queue, I was wanting to know what was on the menu. Burger and chips followed by coconut cake and custard. Oh my god – brilliant. It had to be a quick turnaround if you were in with a chance to get another bit of cake.

"Alright Miss, how are you today?" I said to the dinner lady.

"Alright Jonny, your favourite today," she replied.

"Yeah Miss, you make the nicest cake and custard in the world," I replied.

"Yeah, yeah, Jonny. You say all the right things." As she lifted another bowl with cake and custard and set it under the bench she said, "I hear it's your birthday." She winked at me.

I played along and said, "Yeah Miss, it is."

As I smiled I had caught the attention of Jonty and his henchmen. They turned and said, "Oh Jonny, birthday boy. Great, we will see you outside."

Fuck, I thought. *I'm in for a kicking and all over a bit of bloody cake.*

As I sat there with my mates eating my burger and chips, I thought, *How the fuck am I getting out of this?*

My mind was running wild. Should I make a run for it or just brave it out? Well there was an extra portion of cake and custard with my name on it, and how bad could it be? Couple of smacks maybe.

As I tucked into my second bit of cake, the three stooges walked past Jonty, reached from behind me, and pushed my head into the bowl of custard. "Happy birthday, ball bag," he said.

As I lifted my head, now all dripping with custard, everyone was laughing and pointing.

Bastard, I thought. But what could I do? Those three would knock the bollocks out of me.

One of the dinner ladies came over with a cloth and said to me, "Here, Jonny. Clean yourself up."

"Thanks Miss. I was enjoying that too."

"Don't worry, son. Come back down after school, I have a bit left over for you."

"Thanks Miss, I will see you then." And off I went.

As I walked past the office, a brain wave came to me. "'Scuse me, Miss. I lost my coat on Friday, was it handed in?"

"Don't know, Jonny. Come on in and check the lost and found."

As I rummaged through a big box in the office store, I just wanted a coat to fit, Brilliant – a duffle coat, and it was black as well. I looked around, where I found a pen and quickly wrote my initials on the label.

I looked over my shoulder to make sure nobody had seen and said, "Brilliant Miss, it's here."

As I stood up something caught my eye – the toe of a football boot. I plundered again in the box. Holy fuck, a pair of Umbros and they looked about my size. I opened my school bag up and put them inside; my heart was thumping. A pair of boots, my first pair of boots. As I walked through the office, I said, "Thank goodness, Miss. You couldn't do without a coat in that weather."

I couldn't get out of the office quick enough. I Just got out of the door when I heard, "Jonny, hope them boots fit you as well."

I turned and said, "Thanks Miss, so do I."

You could get away with nothing in our school, or was it just me? I seemed to get caught every time.

I couldn't get the rest of the day in quick enough; 3.25 and the bell went – I was out the door like a rat out of a drainpipe and on the bus home.

I sat beside Billy on the way home and showed him my boots.

"Where'd you get them, mate?" Billy asked.

"In the lost and found, mate. Aren't they weaker?" I replied.

"Look a bit big mate, what size are they?"

"Don't know. mate." As I looked at the label it read 'size 6'. "They're a six, mate. A bit big but beggars can't be choosers," I replied, laughing.

"Yeah mate. Try them bad boys out on Saturday."

Off the bus and a quick dander home, and in through the front door.

"Alright Mum," I said as I threw my bag in the corner, and up the stairs I went to try my new boots on.

I was so excited; pulling on the right boot, then the left, I stood up and yep, they were about two sizes to big but God, they were beaut. My mum came in.

"How was your day, son?" she asked.

I looked over and she noticed my boots and my big grin.

"Where'd you get them fancy shoes, son?" she asked.

"They were in the lost and found in school, Mum. Nobody claimed them so the secretary girl gave me them," I lied through my front teeth. "They are football boots, Mum. Aren't they smashing?" I asked.

"Yeah, son. They are lovely, you will score loads of goals in them."

"I hope so, Mum. Can't wait for Saturday."

The rest of the week was just the same aul crap;

up, school, home, tea, a bit of TV, then bed. Up, school, dodge Jonty and his cronies to avoid getting a beating, and then home. It was like bloody Groundhog Day until Saturday.

CHAPTER 6

Smelly Cat Woman

Work with Nigel and down to Dover Street.

"Alright Nigel, how's the form?" I asked.

"Filled in and sent away," he replied.

Again I laughed at his reply, and off we went to start the run.

One of my calls that day I absolutely hated going to; I nicknamed it Smelly's. She was an old woman who had about ten cats, and they never got out so when I rapped the door it was always the same outcome.

"Come on in, love. The door's open."

A big deep breath, and in I went.

"Hello missus, what would you like today?" I asked, holding my breath, trying not to breathe in.

"Close the door quick in case my babies get out!" she replied.

I was slowly running out of breath as I looked round, and there were cats, bloody everywhere, and cat shit as well. I was now out of breath and had to inhale. Oh my god, the smell was overpowering; I coughed and tears starting running down my face.

"Are you ok, love?" the wee woman asked. "Have you caught that aul cold that's going round?"

"Yeah missus, I have." I was coughing again and the stench was getting worse – I had to get out of there, and quick. "Will I just give you a mixture today?" I asked.

"Yes love, that will do."

I bolted out the front door, gasping for fresh air, and there was Nigel with his window down, laughing.

"Are you alright Jonny?" he asked, laughing his head off.

"Oh my god Nigel, it's bad today. I couldn't breathe in there, there is cat shit everywhere. I can't go back in. You will have to go, Nigel."

"No chance son, it's your call so suck't up and away you go," he replied.

I lifted four mixed bottles; a big deep breath, and in I went.

When I'd closed the door behind me so I didn't let the woman's cats out, doing my best not to breathe in, I said to the woman.

"That's a quid, missus. Where will I put these bottles?"

"In the kitchen, love," she replied.

Holy fuck, I thought. *I'm never going to get out of here alive*. For the brief moments it took me to dodge the cats' shit and set the bottles down on the kitchen table, I had again run out of breath. I did my best not to cough but the smell was burning my nostrils and I started coughing again.

"You may get yourself to McDowell's and get a tonic for that cough before it turns into something more serious," the woman said.

"Yeah missus," I said as I held my hand out for the money and again, another breath and another cough.

"There you go, love," the woman said as she put a pound in my hand.

Again, I dodged the cat shit, and out the door I went, again, gasping for air.

As I got into the van Nigel said to me, "Did you not get the empties?"

I thought to myself, *Not a bloody chance I'm going back in there*. "She hadn't finished them Nigel," I replied.

"Oh right," he said, laughing.

"Your turn next week, Nigel," I said. "I couldn't breathe in there. The floor was covered today."

"Not a chance, Jonny. That's why you get the big wages," he laughed.

I couldn't get that smell out of my nose all day.

We finished the run and I got my wages and said my goodbyes. "See you next week Nigel."

"Yes Jonny. See you then, son."

And I slammed the door shut.

I went straight up the stairs to get changed for the match. Same teams as last week; the banter all week was that we were going to get duffed this week.

Not a chance, I thought. Up against Billy at left back and my new boots, it was going to be easy.

A rap came to the door and my mum shouted up, "Billy is at the door, Jonny."

"Come'n now, Ma."

And out the door I went.

"Be back for your tea, son," my mum said.

"Yeah Ma. See you later."

When we got up to the Woodvale the teams had already set up coats for nets in between the two sets of trees. Stevo shouted at me, "Come on Jonny! Hurry up, we are about to kick off!"

On with my boots and I felt ten feet tall. Nobody was gonna take the ball off me.

We kicked off and straight away Stevo passed the ball out to me. My first touch was awful and Billy took me and the ball. *What the fuck?* I thought as Billy ran up the line, leaving me on my arse.

I had a brutal game, even managed to lose one of my boots as I ran up the line. That got a quare laugh from Billy as he again took the ball off me and called me a muppet.

The game finished 2-0 to the Glencairn ones and I was mostly to blame, kept giving the ball away.

As me and Billy walked down home, he was winding me up.

"You were shit the day," he said.

"I don't know what was wrong, Billy."

"It's them bloody boots, they're too big for you, mate."

"Probably Billy, they are going in the fire when I get home."

"Wise up, Jonny. I will take them, I take a size six."

I handed the boots over to Billy and said, "Hope they bring you more luck than me, mate."

Easy come, easy go, I thought, but I still needed a pair of boots.

I said my goodbyes to Billy and went in through the front door.

CHAPTER 7

My New Boots

My mum was in, cooking dinner. She turned to me. "Alright son, how was the match?"

"Crap, Mum. We got beat two-nil."

"Awk well, son. I take it that's why the long face."

"Yeah Mum, am rage'n. It was my fault. My boots were too big and my touch was awful."

She turned back to the cooker and turned the pots off. She washed her hands and walked over to me.

"Get your coat, son. We are going out."

"Ma, I'm knackered. Where have we to go?"

"Going to get you new boots, now get your coat."

New boots? Oh my god, new boots! I thought. I lifted my coat off the banister and out the door we went.

"Where we going, Ma?" I asked.

"Down the town to SS Moore's, son."

"Mum, that's a dear shop. We couldn't afford boots out of there."

"I'm buying you boots, son, and that's where we are going."

We walked onto the Shankill; it was starting to get dark. My mum flagged a black taxi down. As we got into the taxi my mum said, "Royal Avenue, love."

The taxi man was the biggest man I had ever seen. He was as wide as he was tall; he nearly filled the whole of the front seats.

"Yes love," he replied, and off we went down the road.

"What has yous heading into town at this time? The shops will be closed in half an hour," he asked.

"My son needs a pair of football boots so we are going to Moore's," she replied.

"Oh right, love. Is he any good?" the man asked.

"Yeah he is, he's going to play for Linfield someday."

I was scundered. I nudged my mum. "Mum," I said, going a bit red.

"You are, Jonny. Someday you will play for the wee sons of Ulster."

I could only dream of that day.

The taxi driver pulled over into Royal Avenue and swung the cab round to face back up North Street.

"There you go, love. That's 90p."

My mum reached into her purse and handed the man a quid. "That's ok, love. Keep the change."

We got out of the cab and walked towards the city hall, where SS Moore's was on the corner.

We got into the shop about 4.40, twenty minutes before they closed, and I walked straight over to where the boots were. There were so many different kinds and I lifted a pair of Pumas down – they were magic. I turned them over to see how much they were – forty quid. I exhaled and my heart sunk; I put them back up on the shelf. My mum put her hand on my shoulder.

"They no good, Jonny?"

"No, Ma. I don't like them."

I walked on down to the sale section and there, tucked away under the shelf, I spotted a pair of last season's Pumas, pure black with the famous cat up the side. My heart missed a beat as I turned them over to see how much. Twelve quid – I couldn't believe my eyes – and size four. Perfect. "These, Ma. I want these."

She smiled at me and said, "Ok Jonny, calm down. They're only a pair of boots."

No they weren't. *These are the boots Maradona wore*, I thought, *and I would give my left arm just to have them.*

My mum brought them up to the till and reached into her purse to pay for them. She handed me the bag and said, "There you go, son. Hope they bring you luck."

I threw my arms round her and squeezed really tight. "Thanks Ma, I love them. Thanks."

We walked back up to the taxi rank to get a lift home, and there and behold, it was the fat man again.

We both got in. The man slid the glass partition open and said, "Well what did you get, son?"

I opened the bag and lifted out a boot. "Pumas," I said with a big smile on my face.

"They are belters," he replied. "Good luck with them."

He slid the glass shut and off we went up the Shankill, past the leisure centre, up past Tenant Street. As we drove past the Mountain View bar I saw my da coming out, staggering as he headed for home.

My mum spotted him too and the look on her face said it all. I knew we had to get home before he did or all hell would break loose.

We got off at the Woodvale and took to our heels to get home. I had never seen my mum run as fast in her life, but the threat of my da kicking off was enough for us both to get home in a hurry.

I burst in through the front door and up to my room to hide my boots. My mum was not too far behind me as she went straight into the kitchen to get the dinner back on.

I ran back down the stairs to get the TV on and just as I jumped onto the sofa my da came in through the front door.

"Hello, my wee family," he slurred. "Guess what your da done today?"

I thought, *Just the usual – get bloody drunk*. "What, Da?" I replied.

"Just took 100 quid off the bookies." As he reached into his trousers he pulled out the money he had left.

"Jimmy, that's brilliant. How'd you do it?" my mum asked.

"Four-timer, love. I had three quid on them and they all rumped it. Jonny, here son." He lifted a tenner out. "Away and run down to the shop and give this tenner to Aggie. Tell her to take it off my bill and get six beers off her for me."

I looked at my ma and she said, "Away you go, Jonny. Go and do what your da says."

Away I went down to the shop.

When I returned my da had the record player on and I could hear him sing along to Kenny Rogers and The Gambler.

"Good lad, Jonny," he said as he stretched out his hand to get the beer. "*You got to know when to the fold them*," he sung.

He was in quare form as my mum served the dinner out.

That night was great crack; my ma and da up dancing to my da's records. I even had a dance as well, as mum burled me round to the sounds of Abba.

When the beer was done my da lay down on the sofa and fell asleep. My ma backed the fire in and off to bed we went.

CHAPTER 8

A Trip To Ards

The next morning, when I got up and went into my mum's room she was sitting at the end of the bed and she looked worried.

"What's wrong Mum?" I asked.

"Jonny, Jonny when we got the taxi up home last night and when we saw your da, we were in that big of a rush to get home I forgot to pay the taxi fare."

"Mum, it will be alright. It's only 90p, stop worrying," I replied.

But my mum was as honest as the day was long, and she knew what she had to do.

We had breakfast and my mum kept looking up at the clock. When it was time to go to my nanny's my mum said, "Jimmy, are you going to my mum's?" She knew rightly he wouldn't.

"No love, got a bit of a sore head," he replied, as

he sat in front of the fire puffing his brains out.

"Come on Jonny, get your coat and we will go on down to your nan's."

Out the door and down onto the Shankill we went. We stopped just above Tennett Street and waited for a black taxi to come.

We must have stopped five or six black cabs until we found the fat man. My mum opened the back door and poked her head in.

"I'm so sorry," she said. "I forgot to pay you last night."

"Don't worry love, I knew you were in a rush."

"I do worry, I should of payed you," she replied, as she lifted a quid out of her purse.

"Your money is no good, love." He handed her a piece of paper and a pen. "If your son is that good of a footballer, can he sign this for me?" he asked.

My mum looked confused. "What do you mean?" she asked.

"I want his signature for the fare. You never know, if he becomes famous I want the first autograph."

My mum looked at me and said, "Jonny, sign this for the man."

I was scundered. "What will I write?" I asked the man.

"Can you make it out to Big Sam and just sign your name."

I wrote on the page 'To Big Sam from Jonny Andrews. Thanks for the lift.'

I handed the man the page back and he said to me, "I will put that along with Norman Whiteside's signature. Thanks Jonny."

My mum closed the door and the two of us stood there. I think we were in shock at what had just happened; we both looked at each other and just laughed.

Life was great and the next few days were just the normal events, until Thursday at school, when I was asked to go and play for the school football team. My first chance playing for a proper team – I was buzzing.

Just after lunch we had to meet in the sport hall and when I walked in all the lads were there – Stevo, Davo, Stephen the cat for nets, and Billy my mate. The rest of the lads I didn't really know that well but I knew they were all fourth and fifth years.

Mr Miller, the P.E. teacher, said to me, "Aright Jonny, come on in. We are just having our team talk."

I walked over and Billy patted me on the back.

"I hear you're a wizard on the right wing, Jonny," Mr Miller asked.

"Yeah, I'm alright," I replied.

"You're a weaker," big Stevo said. He was the captain of the team and I looked up to him.

Mr Miller said, "These boys said we have to have you in the squad. Even though you're only in second year, they said we have to get you."

I was well chuffed as we all headed out for the school bus.

"Who are we playing, Billy?" I asked.

"It's the first round of the Schools Cup, we are playing a team from Ards, think you call them Movilla," he replied.

"Oh, right," I replied. I had never left Belfast so I couldn't even tell you were Ards was, never mind a team called Movilla.

We got on the bus and off we went. It took about an hour to get there but we arrived at a place called Londonderry Park and we went into the changing rooms to get our kit on.

Mr Miller named the team to start and he told me I was on the bench, so off we went to start our run in the Schools Cup.

This was the first time I had seen the school team play and wow, they were good. Every tackle, every header we won and by half time we were 3-0 up. During our half-time team talk, Mr Miller said just keep playing like that, and there would be more goals.

I was sure at 3-0 I would get on, but nope, I stood there with my new boots on and didn't even kick a ball.

It finished 5-0 and I couldn't really celebrate. I was raging that I didn't get to play.

We all got on the bus and my face could tell a picture. "What's wrong, Jonny?" Mr Miller asked,

As if he didn't know, I thought as I lifted my head. "Nothing sir," I replied.

"Now Jonny, no huffing. You didn't get on today 'cause I just brought you to get to know the boys and see how we play."

I couldn't even answer him as I fought back the tears; I just nodded and smiled.

"Come to training on Monday and we will get a look at you."

"Ok sir, I will."

I was determined to get on that team and show him what a player I was.

CHAPTER 9

Here Comes Santa

The next day I arrived home from school and walked in the house to be met by two men in black leather coats, and my mum standing there with a worried look on her face. I threw my school bag in the corner. "Hi Mum, who's these men?" I asked.

"Jonny, away up to your room," my mum said worriedly.

And so I walked slowly up the stairs. I had never seen these two men before and was really worried about what was going on. I walked to the top of the stairs and closed my door but crouched down to listen what was going on downstairs.

"Mrs Andrews, we are here for payment," one of the men asked.

"What payment are you talking about?" my mum replied.

"Your Jimmy borrowed 100 quid on Saturday and

it's pay day."

"I don't know what you're talking about but I don't have 100 quid to give you."

"You don't understand, we are here for your first instalment. It's five quid interest and if you want to pay anything off the hundred we will take that off your bill."

Oh my god, that's where my da got the money from on Saturday. Dirty lying pig, I thought. *And he has left my ma to pay for it.*

My mum said to them, "Hold on, I will get you the money," as she walked up the stairs.

Shit. I got up and ran into my room, hoping she didn't see me.

I heard my mum go back downstairs so I crept back out again to hear what was going on.

"Here," my mum said. "Here's your five quid and take twenty quid off the bill."

One of the men said, "Thanks Mrs Andrews, see you next Friday," and they left.

I went downstairs and asked my mum, "What was that about, Ma?"

"Nothing to worry you, son," she replied as she walked into the kitchen and started dinner.

I found out later that it was the U.V.F. and it took my ma about six weeks to pay them back. She never mentioned it to me again or I to her.

I made the school football team and the next couple of games I got to play a bit in them. The second game I started the second half right wing – my favourite position.

We were 1-0 down in the next round of the Schools Cup; we were playing a team from Antrim and they were a big, strong team so it was a tough game.

Mr Miller said to me at half time, "Right, Jonny lad, let's see what you have. You have thirty-five minutes to get us a goal."

My heart was thumping as the whistle sounded to start the second half. Antrim had kick-off and big Stevo lunged into a tackle to win the ball back for us. He passed out to me on right wing and my first touch took me past the left winger and off I went down the right wing. It felt amazing running down the right wing. In came a tackle; I chipped the ball over him and jumped the tackle. I could hear Stevo shout, "Go, Jonny! Go at them!"

I beat the last man and looked up. There was Stevo, standing unmarked in the six yard box. One swift boot and the ball was straight to him and he shot home – one each and game on.

The team all celebrated with him and off we went back into our own half.

We beat Antrim 3-1 that day and I felt like a superstar in my new boots. So that was us into the quarter finals – eight teams left – so the buzz with all the lads was brilliant.

Saturday morning and I had to meet Nigel. It was going to be a really hard day as it was the Saturday before Christmas and we had double run to do.

When I turned up in Dover Street I couldn't believe my eyes at the amount of crates on Nigel's van. How the hell were we going to sell all this lemonade?

"Alright Nigel, that's some load you have on today."

"Yes Jonny, it is, son, but we will get through it, ok? So don't panic."

Off we went. This was my first Christmas run and it was brilliant. The people on the Shankill were really good to me; every call I did gave me either a tip or a gift – they ranged from selection boxes to socks. I even got an out-of-date calendar that day, which me and Nigel had a quare laugh at.

At the end of the day I was shattered and so was Nigel but my pockets were filled and Nigel gave me fifteen quid as well, so I was well-heeled that day, and the gifts, it must have taken me ten minutes to bring them into the house. When I finally got the last one brought in, I wished Nigel a merry Christmas and a happy new year. He asked me to hold on a minute; I was puzzled as he reached into the van, and he brought a box out. He carried it into our house.

"Annie, are you there?" he called.

My mum came out of the kitchen. "Yes Nigel, what is it? I hope our Jonny behaved himself today."

He set the box on the table. "Yes he did, Annie. He was a great help today. Here, this is for you, Annie."

My mum was as surprised as me. "What is it Nigel?"

'Wait till I leave but you have to open it, don't leave it till Tuesday and Christmas Day."

"I will, Nigel." My mum gave Nigel a big hug and

wished him merry Christmas. "Thanks, you're too kind."

"No worries Annie, you and the family have a nice Christmas as well, and tell that Jimmy boy don't be getting too drunk." He laughed and out the door he went.

Me and my mum stood at the front door and waved him off.

We both went back inside and straight to the box which was on the table. We were very excited to find out what was in it.

The suspense was killing me. "Frig's sake, Ma. Open it."

And she did; we both looked inside and it was full of food and household stuff. Nigel even put in a big ham and a Christmas cake. There was a lot of food in it and me and my mum were chuffed to bits (custard, biscuits, tins of soup, a big bar of Dairy Milk – the list was endless and everything in it, we would use).

My mum said to me, "Oh my goodness, Jonny, look at all the presents you got. You will be eating selection boxes till Easter."

I put all my presents under the Christmas tree which was beside the TV. Our wee Christmas was getting exciting – my ma had put all the decorations on the ceiling and our tree was class; our wee house was lovely.

"Jonny, I have your tea on so away up and get yourself changed out of them dirty clothes."

I tramped up the stairs. My legs were like lead weights and my arms were as bad but the thought of counting my tips was keeping me going. Into my room, and I emptied my pockets. All in all I had forty-two quid, so when I added that to what I had saved, oh my god, I was rich – ninety quid. I had never had as much money in my whole life and, now my mind started racing over what to do with it.

"Jonny, your tea's on the table!" my mum shouted up the stairs.

I shoved the money into my tin box and hid it under my bed, threw my jammies on, and headed downstairs.

When I sat at the table, my mum had made stew and big whacks of crusty bread from Ohara's, with real butter and a big glass of milk.

I tore into it and it was beaut – every mouthful heated me up on such a cold night and with the crusty, I mopped up the juice of the stew and horsed it down as well.

I sat and watched a bit of telly but I was that tired I couldn't keep my eyes open, and when I looked up at the clock it was 8 o'clock and I'd had enough – bed for me.

As I gave my mum a kiss goodnight she said to me, "Goodnight son. Three more sleeps till Santa."

"Ma, I'm fourteen, come on."

She laughed and said, "Now Jonny, if you don't believe..."

"Yeah Ma, night-night."

And as I walked up the stairs I couldn't have timed it better. I could hear my da singing Jingle Bells coming down our street. I turned and laughed.

"Here's Santa now, Ma."

And she laughed too. "Too many sherries for him I think, Jonny."

When my head hit the pillow I was out like a light.

CHAPTER 10

The Fight

The next day, I woke up, looked out of the window, and the place was white. Happy days, it had snowed all night. I thought it must have been a foot deep as I threw my clothes on to go out and play in it.

Me and a few of my mates went up to the Woodvale and had a snowball fight with the Glencairn ones, but it only lasted about half an hour, when a few of the lads said, "Come on, we will go to Ardoyne and pelt the Taigs."

It seemed a good idea at the time but things went horribly wrong.

We walked up Twadell Avenue and got to the roundabout. With it being a Sunday and with the heavy fall of snow, there were no cars on the road – it was like one big playground.

But this was no game. The talk was, "Let's get stuck in. Let's break a few windees and do a few cars."

I didn't want to be a chicken so I went along with it.

There were about ten lads from Ardoyne, some of them wearing their Celtic tops, which infuriated the lads more, and so it began.

One snowball was thrown, then it just went nuts and before we knew it, it was a full-blown digging match. There were about twenty of us so at first we kicked the shit out of them, but all of a sudden we were outnumbered and the tide had turned. Two lads got hold of me and were giving me a good going over – punch after punch, kick after kick – and I was in trouble. I tried to get up but kept being punched to the ground. I think I passed out at one stage as I don't remember much after that, but I do remember how cold it was and being dragged through the snow.

When I came round it was Stevo I saw standing over me. He was covered in blood and when I got to my feet I was covered in blood too, and with the snow it looked like a blood bath.

"Jonny! Jonny, are you ok?" Stevo asked.

I got up and looked at him, very dazed and confused. "I think so, mate. Look at the state of you, are you ok?"

The blood was running from his mouth and nose and his top was ripped and covered in blood.

"Never mind that, Jonny. We got to get out of here, the peelers are coming and the bastards are regrouping."

As he pointed over towards Ardoyne, I looked over and it was bedlam; the fighting was nuts, people screaming and shouting and people lying everywhere covered in blood.

Two meat wagons came flying past us with the sirens on and stopped at the roundabout, the peelers piled out of the back of them and started hammering anyone in their way. That was our cue to get off side.

As we walked down Twaddell Avenue I lifted a handful of snow and held it to my face to try and numb the pain. We started talking about what had just happened and Stevo said to me, "Fuck, didn't that go wrong. We got hammered there, I hope the other lads got away."

"Yeah Stevo, I hope they're ok," I replied as I lifted another handful of snow and started trying to clean myself up. "My ma's going to kill me, Stevo. Look at the state of me." My coat was gone, my top ripped to bits, my jeans were covered in blood, and I was missing a shoe.

"I know, mate. My da's gonna crack too, but what can we do? We are just going to have to face the music."

As we walked down past the Woodvale a crowd of men came walking up carrying baseball bats and iron bars. They stopped us and started asking questions.

"Yous lads ok?"

Stevo replied, "Not really, but we we'll live."

One of the men put his arm round me. "You're Jimmy's lad aren't you?"

"Yes mister, I am."

"We are going up to sort them bastards out."

The men walked on and me and Stevo kept walking towards the Shankill road.

"I'm glad, Stevo, we aren't back up at Ardoyne. Somebody gonna get killed up there if the men get them."

"That's the U.V.F., Jonny, and yes, someone gonna get it. Fuck, Jonny we started that. What are we going to do?"

"Nothing mate, we are lucky to be still standing so I hope they do get stuck into them. It will serve them right."

I told Stevo I was going home and that I would see him later in the week.

As I walked up Broom Street I was trying to make an up excuse for my mum about what had happened. I was really scared of what she was going to say.

I opened the front door and my mum was sitting at the table reading a book. She looked at me.

"Oh my god. Jonny, what happened?"

"I was in a fight, Ma."

"With who, Jonny? Oh my god, son, you're in a bad way."

She went straight into the kitchen and put the kettle on and lifted a tea towel. "Come here, son. Let's get you cleaned up."

As she got a basin out from beneath the sink she put some bottle of stuff in it and poured some hot water from the kettle in.

She dampened the tea towel and started wiping my face.

"Shit. Ma, that stings. What is it?"

"Dettol, Jonny. It will smart but it will clean any dirt away."

She wiped again. I don't know what was worse, the cuts or the bloody Dettol.

Tears started running down my face as the pain got worse.

"Jonny, son, take your top off."

I struggled to lift the tee-shirt over my head, my back and ribs were aching and more tears rolled down my cheeks. I was black and blue, I had taken a real kicking.

"Awk, Jonny look at the state of you. Who done this to you?" she asked.

"Ma, we went up to Ardoyne to have a snowball fight with the Taigs but it ended up a fight."

"What have I told you before, stay away from up there," she said, as she wiped the back of my head and the blood away.

As I looked at my mum she was crying too.

"Ma, it's ok. I'm alright, stop crying."

"You're not, Jonny." She put her arms round me to give me a hug.

I winced as she hugged me with the pain in my ribs.

"Sorry Jonny. Sorry son."

As she loosened her grip.

"It's ok, Ma. Just a bit sore."

"Away up and get your jammies on, son. I will get

you a couple of painkillers."

I walked up the stairs and into my room, the tears still running down my cheeks. I sat on my bed and struggled to pull my jeans off; every movement was agony. I was really sobbing as my door opened and my da was standing there.

"You ok, son? Your ma was telling me what happened."

I wiped the tears from my cheeks and said, "Aye, Da. I'm ok."

"Come on, I'll help you on with your jammies, son."

I stood up after putting my bottoms on and my da helped me on with my top.

"You're lucky to be home, son. There is murder up at Ardoyne. Someone told me there is two dead and six peelers injured."

The realisation of what could have happened hit me.

"Da, me and my mates started it but it was only a snowball fight."

"No, son. Nobody deserves this," he said as he rubbed my head. "Come on down and we will get some tea."

As I struggled to walk downstairs my da lifted me and carried me down, and set me on the sofa.

He sat beside me. "Son, promise me you won't go back up there, even just for a nosey."

"I will, Da. I won't go back."

My mum came over with a glass of water and two tablets. "Here, Jonny. Take these, it will help with the pain."

I swallowed the tablets and handed her the empty glass. "Thanks Ma."

As I sat there in front of the fire, watching the TV, my da put his arm round me. "You ok, son?"

I hadn't sat with my da like this in a long time; it felt safe, and I just cuddled into him. "Yeah, Da. I'm ok."

I fell asleep in his arms and couldn't remember the next morning how I got to bed. My da must have carried me up.

Monday and Christmas Eve, I got out of bed and was bloody sore all over. I went into the bathroom and looked in the mirror; not too bad, bit of a black eye and a busted lip. *That Dettol must be good stuff*, I thought.

I walked downstairs and my ma and da were sitting at the table. There was big plate of toast and a plate of sausages with three cups of tea.

I pulled a chair out and sat down. Nobody said a word.

It felt like ages before my da said, "Two lads died yesterday, son. Up at Ardoyne."

My heart was pumping. "Who, Da? Who?"

"Don't know, son, but they came from up the road."

Oh my god. My mind was racing and my heart was thumping right up into my throat.

A knock came to the door; my da went and answered it.

Some man was standing there in a black leather jacket. I recognised him – it was the same guy who collected the money for the U.V.F.

"Jimmy, was your Jonny up at Ardoyne yesterday?"

"Aye, he was. Why do you need to know?" my da replied.

I was shitting myself. "What's wrong, mister?" I asked.

He looked at me. "It's ok, son. We are checking if you're ok. There is a few lads still missing."

"Who got killed, mister?"

"We can't say until we see all the parents, son, but we can account for you now."

I stood there with my head in my hands and cried. My mum stood up and hugged me. "It's ok, Jonny. It's ok, son."

The man left and my da closed the door. He came over and hugged me as well. As the three of us stood in our living room hugging, we all were crying. I had never seen my da cry before and it was terrible. I swore to myself that day that I would never get involved in fighting with the Taigs again as I could have been one of those lads that lost their lives in what started out as a bit of crack.

*

Christmas that year was terrible; none of my family or friends had any heart to celebrate it. I was sore for a few days and never left the house.

It turned out that the two lads killed that day were from Glencairn, both were sixteen. I only knew them from playing football up in the Woodvale; they had left school so I only saw them now and again.

The funerals of the boys took place on the Friday and my family and I went.

I wore my school uniform and my ma and da were dressed in black. As we left our house at ten in the morning to walk up to Glencairn, it was raining and I got under the umbrella with my mum. As we walked past Twadell Avenue I recalled the fighting and a real chill went down my spine at how lucky I was; today could have been my funeral. I held my mum's hand a little bit tighter and she squeezed my hand back. I looked up at her and she smiled. "You ok, son?" she asked.

"Aye, Ma," I replied, but I wasn't really. I was shaking with fear as I recalled being kicked and punched only a couple of hundred yards away.

We got up to the church halfway up Glencairn Road and the crowds of people turned the road black. There must have been 1,000 people there that morning and a lot of sad faces as I looked round to see if any of my mates were there.

I spotted Stevo standing with his mum, dad, and sister. I nodded over and he nodded back. We both stared at each other for a brief moment and I'm sure he was thinking the same as me. *That could be us lying in them coffins.*

As the coffins were being carried out of the church, overwhelming sadness fell over the crowd and a lot of the people were crying as well as myself. I just hung onto my mum, and my dad put his arm round me and held me tight.

I couldn't wait till get home and back to the safety of our living room.

CHAPTER 11

The Schools Cup Final

The Christmas holidays dragged by and I couldn't wait to get back to school and back to normal, so I was glad to be on the bus on Monday, seeing all my mates again.

The talk on the bus was still about the two lads that lost their lives, and one lad I even heard boast about fighting. I turned my head to hear what he was saying.

"I smacked the first one and his nose just exploded all over his face. He never got up again so I stuck the boot into him and got stuck into the next one. I must of knocked three out before they got a dig in. When the peelers came they had to drag me off one. I was gonna kill him but the fuckers got me off him."

Stevo looked at me and shook his head. "Don't say anything, Jonny. He's nuts, he will kill you."

I just nodded and turned my head back.

When we got off the bus I said to Stevo, "I never seen him up at Ardoyne, did you?"

"No, mate. He's talking crap, he wasn't there."

"I knew that, mate. So why is he talking shit?"

"To make himself look like a big man," Stevo replied.

We walked into school and to our reg classes. "See you later, Stevo," I said.

"Aye, mate. See you at lunch."

After a few classes I wished I had still been off and in the house. School was boring as hell and I had three years of this left to do.

*

A few weeks passed and we had made the final of the Schools Cup – it was to be played at Seaview, the home of Crusaders Football Club. It was a Friday night 7pm kick-off and we were to play St. Pat's, a real tough team, and to make it worse, a Catholic team from the other side of town.

The squad was to meet at 5pm back up at school and I was sick with nerves. I was now fifteen playing for the under sixteens' team and all these lads were like monsters to me. They were huge. Big Stephen the cat was like man mountain; there was no way you would say boo to him, never mind go and challenge for the ball. Then you had our defenders, they looked like a line-up from Crimewatch; they all had skinheads and were built like brick shit houses. Our midfield was Stevo and Jonty in centre-mid; they were two hard tickets as well. Jimbo played left wing and Paul was out on the right. Our two centre forwards were big – Gary, he must have been 6ft tall, and wee Mickey, he wasn't much bigger than me but tough as nails. We had three subs – Ross, Frankie, and myself.

When I walked into the canteen we were all told to sit round two tables that were put together. Mr Miller said, "Alright lads, how are we all? Anybody any injuries?"

Everyone replied, "No sir, all good."

Just at that, two of the dinner ladies came out of the kitchen with trollies and plates of food on them. They started handing them out and my eyes lit up; fish and chips – brilliant.

As we all sat round the tables, the crack was brilliant. Even Mr Miller got a turn as Birtie, our centre half, said to him, "Here, sir, I hear you have a thing for Miss Patterson."

All the lads laughed as Mr Miller replied, "No, Birtie. It's your ma a fancy."

We all laughed even louder. I looked over at Birtie as he replied, "My ma would knock your bollocks in, sir."

"You're probably right, Birtie. I feel sorry for your da."

We all had a quare laugh sitting there eating our fish and chips.

About 5.30, we got on the bus to make the short journey down to the Shore road and Mr Miller handed out bottles of water. "Get them into you, lads. Make sure you drink the heap."

When we arrived down at Seaview, we walked into the ground and onto the pitch. There were a few people in the stands and there a few reporters there as well.

One of the men came over with a cameraman and he went straight to Mr Miller. I heard him ask him about the match.

"Well, Jimmy, are all the boys up for this tonight?"

"Our boys are ready, we should do ok."

"What about St. Pat's? Did you do your homework?"

"We don't need to worry about them, they need to worry about us."

Stevo had told me four of the St. Pat's team were signed for Liverpool and that their goalkeeper was on Cliftonville's books.

As we walked across the pitch I was really nervous, but Stevo came over and said, "Jonny, stop panicking. You're on the bench, it's us lads under pressure."

"Aye, ano Stevo, but look at the size of the pitch – it's massive."

"It's alright mate, we will be fine," he replied, and we walked into the changing room.

We all sat down and Mr Miller came in, and threw the kit bag on the floor.

"Right lads, get changed as I name the starting line-up."

As expected, I was on the bench along with Frankie and Ross.

When we walked out onto the pitch we were greeted with a huge cheer. As I looked over to the stand it was bunged and my heart started thumping. Mr Miller got us all in and we did a few stretches and a few runs to get warmed up, and we were ready.

St. Pat's lined up in their green and white hoops with green shorts and socks. We were in a white top with a red stripe down one side, with red shorts and socks. We all shook hands and got set for kick-off.

As the ref blew his whistle a loud cheer came from the crowd and the game started.

I watched on as the tackles flew in from both sides and free kick after free kick was given. The ref constantly tried to stamp his authority on the game but these were two sides determined to win and I thought to myself, *If one of them St. Pat's lads hit me with a tackle, they would break my leg.*

The first half came to an end with St. Pat's being on top, and if not for Stephen the cat in nets, we could have been two or three down.

We went back into the changing rooms and Mr Miller handed out cut oranges as he gave the team talk.

"Come on lads, we are showing them too much respect. We have to pick up the second balls and when we have it we need more options for the guy on the ball. The movement is rubbish – Stevo, you need to win the midfield battle, your man is getting it too easy."

"I know, sir, but they are playing three in there. We need to drop Gary back in to give me a hand."

"Good idea, Stevo. Gary, you pick the eight up, he's their ball winner. Hit him a hard tackle as soon as you can."

"No problem, sir. I won't let you down," Gary replied.

"Defence, you need to get out quicker. We are keeping them onside when the ball is played back in."

Our defence were hard as anything but they weren't gifted with pace so they all looked at each other in bemusement.

Stevo asked, "Any changes, sir?"

"No, Stevo, not yet. We will give it ten minutes."

My head dropped. I had heard those words before and knew I was going to be a spectator.

The second half started much the same as the first, but five minutes in, the number eight from St. Pat's won the ball in midfield and Big Gary hit him with such a tackle the lad screamed in pain and the ref blew his whistle. Four or five players ran in from both sides, and a lot of slabbering and pushing took place. The ref blew his whistle a few times to separate the two sides and called on the coach from St. Pat's to treat the lad lying on the pitch rolling around in pain.

The ref then called Gary over and issued him a straight red card and pointed to the changing rooms. Mr Miller went nuts, shouting, "Ref! Ref! How's it red? He hardly touched him, the eight dived."

The ref just looked over and shook his head. I think Mr Miller was the only person in the whole ground who didn't see Gary empty him.

That was us down to ten men and we were up against it. Mr Miller kept looking down at me and looking at his watch.

Chance after chance St. Pat's created, but save

after save, Stephen kept them out, and with fifteen minutes to go, Mr Miller turned to me.

"Right Jonny, let's go and win this. You're going on left wing."

"But sir, I usually play on the right."

"I know, son, but when you get on the ball cut in and go for goal."

My heart was thumping as the ball went out and the linesman called the ref to get me on.

As I ran onto the pitch I heard a voice from the crowd. "Go on, Jonny! Go and show them!"

I recognised the voice. I turned and looked up; my mum and dad were near the front of the stand. I gave them the thumbs up and I was ten feet tall. This was the first time my ma and da had seen me play.

St. Pat's took their throw-in and Jonty made the tackle. He passed to Stevo in midfield who got hit by the eight with a real dirty tackle from behind, and the ref blew his whistle again. Pushing and shoving took place; Stevo jumped up and pushed the eight in the chest. He fell like Goliath and rolled around holding his face. The crowd started shouting, "Off! Off! Off! Off!" as the ref blew his whistle another few times.

The ref called Stevo over as the eight got to his feet. *Oh my god*, I thought, *he's gonna send him off.*

Stevo stood there with his arms out, saying, "I didn't touch him, ref. He's cheating."

The ref reached into his pocket and pulled out a yellow card.

"Yes!" I said, clenching my fist, and then he called

the eight over. He reached into a different pocket and showed him a red card. *Brilliant,* I thought. *He's been at it all night. He deserved to go.*

The ref pointed to the changing room as the St. Pat's manager shouted on. "You're a cheat, ref. Are your eyes painted on?"

The ref was only about twenty feet away and walked straight over to him. He pointed to the stand and told him he had to go; the man went nuts and two other coaches had to pull him away. I saw the flash of cameras as photographers took pictures of what was going on. The crowd went nuts; half of them were cheering and half were booing. It must have taken five minutes to get everyone calmed down.

Stevo took the free kick and passed to Ross up front; he squared the ball to me and I started running down the left wing. The ball was stuck to my feet and I cut in and saw Stevo on the edge of the box. I passed and he shot first time. The keeper scrambled across his line and tipped the ball past the post; that was our first real chance as the crowd clapped and we had a corner.

The ball was crossed in and Jonty narrowly missed, but we were in the game now and St. Pat's were worried. They had lost their play maker and their manager.

Two minutes to go and it looked like extra time. I picked the ball up, facing my own goal. Just on the halfway line, I looked over my shoulder and saw the St. Pat's player coming; one flick with my right boot and I span, and left the defender for dead. I ran on with the ball at my feet. Thirty yards... twenty yards...

into the box, and I heard Stevo shout, "Shoot, Jonny! Shoot!"

As I cocked back my right leg to shoot, in came the right back and sent me flying in the air. I landed with such a thump on my back as I heard the ref blow his whistle. I heard a big cheer come from my team and the crowd – the ref had given the penalty.

I got to my feet and Stevo and a few of the lads were hugging me. I looked over and the ref had sent the St. Pat's player off as well. He turned to where we were and said, "Who's hitting the pen, lads?"

Mr Miller shouted over, "Stevo, you hit it."

Stevo went over and lifted the ball. He walked straight over to me and handed me the ball. "It's yours, Jonny. Makers, takers."

"Stevo, I can't. Miller will crack, you hit it."

"No, mate. You're taking it. Never mind about Miller, go and win this."

I turned and looked over at Mr Miller; he threw a water bottle on the ground and turned his back. I then looked over at the crowd, they were going nuts. I don't know why but I lifted the badge of my shirt and kissed it. The crowd cheered and I turned and walked to the penalty spot. I sat the ball down amidst the booing of the crowd behind the net and turned to get my distance right from the ball.

The ref made sure everyone was out of the box and he blew his whistle. I started running to the ball; all I could hear was the beat of my heart – *thump, thump, thump, thump* – my legs were like jelly but as I dressed the ball I struck it with such venom, like my life depended on it, and top bins, the keeper had no chance. I turned to see my teammates run towards me; they all piled on and the cheers from the crowd were deafening. The ref blew his whistle for full time and we had won it.

My teammates lifted me up and ran up the pitch; even Mr Miller was going nuts on the line. Some people from the crowd were on the pitch. I was looking out for my ma and da but there was too much going on, I couldn't see them.

After about five minutes we had all calmed down we were asked to go and receive our winners' medals. I was chuffed to bits. Stevo, our captain, went last and he received the cup. He lifted it aloft to the cheers of the crowd and all the lads included me started singing, "We are champion, we are champions." We were all jumping up and down during the celebrations. A man walked over to me, he introduced himself as Mr Spence. He said, "Hello Jonny, you played a big part in that match. Could I ask you what age you are?"

"Fourteen, mister. Why?" I replied.

"I am the manager of the county team that we are putting together. It's an under sixteen team but I feel you are good enough to be involved."

I was dumbstruck; I didn't know what to say. At that, Mr Miller came over.

"Can I help you mate?" he asked the man.

"I was just saying to Jonny here that I would like him to try out for the under sixteen county squad if that is ok with you."

"Of course it is, that's a great opportunity for the

lad. When and where?"

"Next Sunday, 2pm at the Dub."

I stood there, not knowing what to say. *How the hell am I getting to Dublin?* I thought.

Mr Miller and Mr Spence shook hands and I heard Mr Miller say to Mr Spence, "I will have him there."

We all went into the changing rooms, still singing when we got in. Stevo had lifted a bottle of water and soaked everyone. It was brilliant, we were the Schools Cup winners. I was proud as anything and the youngest player to have played that night.

When I got home my mum and dad were already there and as I walked through the front door the two of them cheered. I smiled from ear to ear. My da said, "You're a footballer alright, son. You were superb, well done," as he patted me on the back.

"Thanks Da, I really enjoyed it."

My mum handed me a big glass of Coke and a sausage sandwich. "Well done, son. I'm really proud of you. Them boots you have are definitely lucky boots." And she smiled; she stood there, beaming.

"Thanks Ma, but you will never guess what happened. I got a trial for the county team but I have to go to Dublin."

"What? Dublin? Why the hell Dublin?" my da asked.

"I was asked to go to the Dub for 2pm next Sunday."

My ma and da started laughing.

"What's so funny?" I asked.

"The Dub is near Taughmonagh, son, not Dublin, you edgit," my da replied.

We all stood there laughing.

I couldn't sleep that night, I was still buzzing with the match, so the next day working for Nigel was a long, tiring day and I couldn't wait till get finished and get home to my bed. I was absolutely shattered.

CHAPTER 12

Gerrerd And The Counties

I couldn't wait until the following Sunday. I met Mr Miller at the corner of Tennett Street at 1pm, and off we went to the Dub.

"Alright Jonny?" Mr Miller asked as we drove down the Shankill in his big flash car.

"Yes sir, this is a nice car you have. What is it?" I asked.

"It's a Ford Escort, son. Why do you ask?"

"Nothing, sir. It's a cracker, how fast does it go?"

"Wouldn't know, son. It's my pride and joy, no way I would rake the life out of her."

"Oh right, sir." *I thought to myself, if I had a car like this I'd have it up the road sidewards with the music thump'n.*

It wasn't long until we arrived at the Dub and before I got out of the car Mr Miller said to me, "Listen Jonny, don't be nervous about this trial. You are a smash'n player and they will be lucky to have you."

I looked at Mr Miller and smiled and said, "I'm not, sir. I'm really excited about playing."

We both got out of the car and walked up to the changing rooms where Mr Spence was standing with a clipboard.

"Alright Jonny lad, you are in changing room two. Your skip is in there and the rest of your team you're playing right wing."

"Thanks sir." And off I went into the building.

When I opened up the door of changing room two there were about twelve players already getting changed. I looked over to where there was a kit hanging and walked towards it. I set my bag on the floor.

Either side of me there was one fellow with ginger hair and on the other side a lad with a skinhead. I said, "Alright lads, how's it going?"

The lad with the ginger hair looked at me and replied, "Alright mate, not too bad. What's your name?"

"Jonny, what's yours?"

"Gerrerd, mate. What position do you play?" he asked.

"Right wing," I replied.

Just at that, the skinhead looked at me. "Don't think so, wee lad. I play right wing."

I didn't know what to say. Gerrerd replied, "I play right back but nobody here is safe in any positon so just do your best."

The thought of going up against this skinhead for the same position was frightening. I really wanted it but was he gonna kick the shit out of me just so I wouldn't get it?

When we were all changed Mr Spence came in. "Sit down lads and I will tell you what's expected. Every one of yous here will get two trials, and if you make the shortlist you will be called back for a third."

I looked round the room and the realisation hit me again. I was the bloody smallest player and probably the youngest, but sure I was here anyway, might as well give it a go.

Mr Miller then said, "When we go out here we will do a fifteen-minute warm up and then go into a match against Linfield under sixteen team."

Holy shit, we were to play Linfield and they were seventeen. I sat there, numb, and didn't really hear what Mr Miller was saying, it was just noise. Then all the lads got up and started heading out.

It was a short walk to the pitch and there was a lot of people all standing watching. I spotted Mr Miller and he waved over. I gave him the thumbs up as I walked onto the pitch with my red football top that was about two sizes too big, and shorts that covered my knees. But on a plus note, my boots fitted.

There were two guys standing and they had set up cones. "Right lads, split yourselves in two teams and line up here," one said as he pointed to two red cones.

We did various drills to get warmed up but I couldn't take my eyes off the Linfield team. They were in the usual blue top, white shorts with red socks, and they looked superb. *What a team,* I thought.

Mr Spence came over after about fifteen minutes and named the starting eleven. He named the various positions, but when he got to right wing my ears pricked up.

The skinhead looked at me. Well, looked down at me – he was head and shoulders above me.

"Jonny Andrews, you're on the right." I heard my heart thump. The skinhead just scowled over at me as he was to start on the bench.

The match kicked off and it was tight at first. Linfield moved the ball really well and cut our defence open on a number of occasions, but at half time it was 2-0 to them and we hadn't had a clear-cut chance.

At half time Mr Spence took me off and the skinhead was put on. He pushed past me as the team went on to start the second half. "You're crap," he said under his breath as he walked past me.

I was raging but Gerrerd said to me, "Don't worry about him, he's just a thug. You never got the ball enough in that half but you done well."

"Thanks mate," I replied.

As I sat on the bench watching the game, our squad was still struggling to gain possession and ten minutes in, Linfield scored again to make it 3-0.

Mr Spence was busy taking notes and I just thought to myself, *I need to be on that pitch if I'm to get a chance at a call back.*

The left back from Linfield picked the ball up and started running down the wing; the big skinhead lunged into a waist-high challenge and really hurt the lad. The ref blew his whistle and gave the foul but he shouted over to Mr Spence, "Change him, he's finished!"

The skinhead gave the ref dog's abuse, effing and blinding. Mr Spence shook his head and looked at me. "Go on, son. You're going on again."

"Ok sir, no problem," I replied as I walked back onto the pitch past the skinhead, who was still cursing his head off.

The ref blew his whistle for the restart and the ball was whipped in. Our keeper rose and caught the ball; he instantly threw the ball to Gerrerd, who took a great touch to go past the left winger. He passed the ball to me and I dragged the ball in one movement as the defender slid in to make the challenge. I ran down the line and whipped the ball into the box; the keeper came and punched the ball but it fell to our centre forward who slotted home – 3-1 – we were back in it.

Fifteen minutes to go and it was all us. Time after time I beat the left back; he couldn't handle me and I was buzzing. Everything I tried came off but it was with five minutes to go I cut inside and struck the ball with my right foot and beat the keeper to make it 3-2.

The game finished and I was chuffed with my performance. As all the lads walked into the changing room, Gerrerd walked in with me. "You played well, Jonny. That was a smasher you scored, you will definitely get called back."

"Thanks Gerrerd, you had a good game too. You're a really strong defender."

"Thanks Jonny."

We both got changed and went outside where Mr Spence was standing with a clipboard he was talking with his two coaches as he looked over to me.

"Jonny Andrews, come over here, son."

My heart was thumping as I walked over. Mr Spence raised his head from the clipboard. "You played well, son, when you came back on. We definitely would like you to come back next Sunday, same time, as we need to get another look at you."

"Thanks sir, I will be here."

As I walked away I felt ten feet tall. Mr Miller was already in his car waiting for me. As I opened the door to get in I heard a voice from behind me. "Jonny, where do you live?"

As I turned, Gerrerd was standing there. "Shankill," I replied.

"Any chance your da could give me a lift?"

"He's not my da, this is Mr Miller, my school teacher."

Mr Miller leaned over. "Where you going, son?" he asked.

"Ardoyne but the Shankill will do, I can walk from there."

Mr Miller replied, "Aye, son. Jump in."

As we drove towards the city centre I was lost for words; my brain was running wild. I couldn't even think of the match, all I could think of was what if anyone saw Gerrerd with me – a Taig from Ardoyne. I would be dead. The closer we got to the Shankill the worse it got. I felt physically sick, the sweat was running down my back.

Then a hand came from the back and Gerrerd had put his hand on my shoulder. "You got a call back, Jonny. So did I, I'm absolutely buzzing – can't wait. If we get picked we are going to the Milk Cup and maybe play against Man U or Leeds. What about you, mate?"

Mate? I thought. *Is he daft? If we are seen together we are both fucked. What am I gonna do?*

"Mr Miller, is that right? Man U or Leeds we will play against?" I asked.

"Yes son, it's a massive chance for you boys, maybe get picked up by one of the scouts. It could be a big opportunity for you both."

I turned to Gerrerd. He was sitting back in his seat, bright ginger hair and a big grin on his face.

"Didn't know that, Gerrerd. Friggin' hell, I love Man U. Who do you follow?"

"Man U as well, mate."

As the car drove up the Shankill I thought to myself that me and Gerrerd were no different, in fact we were very similar and only lived about half a mile from each other.

Mr Miller pulled the car over at Tennett Street and we both got out. I poked my head into the car. "Thanks Mr Miller for the lift, I will see you tomorrow in school."

"No problem son, you done well today."

Gerrerd thanked him as well and we started walking up the Shankill.

"Do you go to the boys' model?" Gerrerd asked.

"Yes mate, I do. What school do you go to?"

"St. Pat's. I hate school, full of dickheads. I can't wait to get out of it and get a job, what about you? Do you like your school?"

"Yeah, it's alright. I just try and keep my head down and dodge the head cases."

Gerrerd laughed. "Every school has them, mate. Do you have many mates outside school?" Gerrerd asked.

I wondered to myself where this was going.

"Not really. One or two older lads I run about with but they leave school this year so don't know what's going to happen."

I didn't want to say too much as my mates hated Taigs, especially ones from Ardoyne.

"Oh right, mate. I don't run about with the headers in our estate, all they want to do is fight with the Woodvale ones and get a riot going with the police. My ma and da would kill me if they caught me out rioting."

Shit, I thought. *That's my mates from the Woodvale he's talking about.*

"Me too, mate. I just keep myself to myself, I don't want to get caught up in that shit, love my football too much."

We walked up the Woodvale; about halfway up Gerrerd said to me, "Where do you live? I take it it's about here somewhere?"

"No mate, I live down in Broom Street about five

minutes back that way," I replied as I pointed down towards the Shankill.

"Why you walking up this way then?"

"Thought I would walk you up a bit," I replied.

"Oh right, sure, this will do. Can you ask Mr Miller could he give me a lift next Sunday if it's not too much trouble?"

"Yeah, will do, it should be sweet. Sure, I will tell him to pick us up at Tennett Street, the Crumlin Road end if that's ok with you?"

I thought, *Less chance of my mates seeing me with Gerrerd and probably safer for him meeting there instead of walking down the Shankill.*

"Spot on, Jonny. That's perfect – 1 o'clock it is, then."

As I said goodbye I turned and started walking home. He was dead on, I was surprised that he was. I always thought boys my age from Ardoyne were scumbags and they probably thought the same of me and my mates.

I walked in the front door and my mum had just put the dinner out. Winner, winner, chicken dinner.

"It's not Christmas, Ma. What's with the big dinner?"

"It's your favourite. Never mind that, how'd you get on today?"

"I have to go back next Sunday for another match. I scored one today but we got beat by Linfield – they were brilliant."

"That's super, son. I'm very proud of you."

As I got tucked into my dinner, it was beaut. Couldn't eat it quick enough.

"Where's my da, Mum?"

"Where do you think? In the bar as usual, he should be home soon."

Aye right, he will only be home when he runs out of money or people to buy him a drink.

"Speak of the devil, there he is," my mum said as my da came through the front door. I turned round to see what state he was in. *Not too bad,* I thought.

"Alright son. Well, did you get a call back?"

"Aye Da, I did, and guess what? If I get picked I'm going to the Milk Cup in July to play against Man U."

"Brilliant, son. I hope you do."

As he sat down beside me and started on his dinner, he looked at me and said, "I'm really proud of you, son. Stay away from the drink and work hard if you really want to be a footballer, then don't let anything or anybody get in your way."

As I sat there I was chuffed to bits. My da had never said anything like that to me before. *He must be full drunk*, I thought.

The next week flew in and at half 12 on Sunday I left the house and headed up Tennett Street to meet Gerrerd and Mr Miller to go for my second trial. As I got to the top of the street I spotted Gerrerd sitting on a wall; his big mop of ginger hair was a pure give away. I crossed the road and sat beside him. "Alright Gerrerd, what's the crack with you?"

"Nothing much, mate. What's the crack with you?"

"Just the usual crap, mate. I was working yesterday with the lemonade man."

"Who?" Gerrerd asked.

"Nigel, our lemonade man. I help him on a Saturday."

"Sweet, is the wages good?" he asked.

"Not bad, mate. Always end up with about fifteen quid with my tips an' all."

"Frig, I would give my left nut for a job like that. You're a lucky man, Jonny."

Just at that, Mr Miller pulled up in his car and off we went to the Dub.

When we arrived it was the usual format, Mr Spence named the team and I was to start right wing and Gerrerd right back. We were to play a team called Bangor FC u17s.

It was an easy game. I ran amuck on right wing, couldn't believe how much time I had on the ball. We won 5-1 and I got on the score sheet again. After the match Mr Spence wanted to speak to everyone separately.

Name after name was called out and each lad left the changing room. It must have been a good twenty minutes and I was still sitting there; five lads remained and I was getting really nervous, I wanted this so bad.

One of the coaches came in. "Jonny, you're next."

I lifted my bag and out I went. Mr Spence was sitting at a table in one of the other changing rooms. I smiled as I went in.

He lifted his head from an open book. "Alright

Jonny, I have a few questions for you and I'm sure you have a few for me."

Shit, it was like being back in school and aul Billy's class. I was crapping myself.

"It was a hard choice today, son. You were up against a couple of bigger, stronger lads for right wing, and the other coaches think you might not be the right choice. What do you think?"

I don't know what came over me but I just started talking. "I might not be the biggest player on the pitch but there is a six-foot giant inside me wanting to get out, and if you put me on the squad I won't let you down, sir. My skills will out play any player you put me up against."

Where the hell did that come from? I shut my mouth and waited for Mr Spence's reply. "That's what I thought, son. I'm backing you 100 percent. I think you're a smashing player, son, and could go all the way, but there is a couple of things I need you bring me next Saturday morning – a birth certificate and fifty quid for your gear and trip to Coleraine. You're going to the Milk Cup, son."

I shook Mr Spence's hand and thanked him for giving me this opportunity. "I won't let you down, sir," I said.

"I know you won't," he replied, and I walked out of the room. My head was buzzing. *I made it. I made it,* I thought.

As I walked over to Mr Miller's car, Gerrerd was already sitting in the back seat. He didn't look happy. Mr Miller said to me, "Well, Jonny? Did you get in?

"Yes sir, I did," I replied with a huge grin on my face. I got into the back of the car and sat beside Gerrerd.

"Well mate, did you get in?" I asked.

"Yes mate, I did, but I can't go."

"What? What do you mean you can't go?"

"I can give you fifty reasons why I can't. Where the hell am I getting fifty quid from for next Saturday? I have no chance."

Shit, I thought. I was that excited I forgot about the fifty quid, and next Saturday, what was I going to do about Nigel as well? That knocked the smile off my face.

"Same boat, mate?" Gerrerd asked.

As we both sat in the back of Mr Miller's car we never spoke a word. Mr Miller pulled the car over. "What's wrong, lads? You would think you two are on your way to your own funerals. You both just made the county squad, do you not realise what that means?"

I lifted my head. "It doesn't matter, sir. We can't go. We have to have fifty quid for next Saturday. We have no chance of getting that sort money in under a week."

"Ask your mums, I'm sure they will pay it for you."

Me and Gerrerd looked at each other. We didn't need to say anything, we both knew that we had no chance; our families just about got by, never mind give us fifty quid for football.

"Lads, if you want this you will get the money. Get

your heads together and work it out."

Mr Miller dropped us off at Tennett Street and we both sat on the wall for a while, talking.

"Do you think you can get the money, Gerrerd?"

"I don't know, mate. I will ask my ma when I get home. What about you?"

"Same boat, mate. We have to. This is our chance, we just have to."

As we said our goodbyes we arranged to meet next Saturday to go and pay the fifty quid.

I walked really slow down Tennett Street, dragging my feet, wondering about the fifty quid. I knew in my tin I had about twenty but was still short. What was I going to do? I walked through the front door – my chin was nearly on the floor. My mum was there to meet me; she put her arm round me.

"Awk well, Jonny. Don't worry, there is always next year."

With tears in my eyes I replied, "I got in, Ma, but I'm short thirty quid. I have only twenty and I need to pay fifty for next Saturday for my trip and gear."

"What? You got in?" My ma burled me round. "You got in! You got in!" She threw her arms round me and hugged me. "That's brilliant, son. Brilliant."

"But Ma, what about the money?"

"We will get the money, son. You're going."

Just at that, my da came down from upstairs. "Did I hear that right? You got selected, son?"

"Yes Da, I did," I replied.

"Well that calls for a celebration. Annie, crack a beer open, our Jonny is going to be a star."

My da put his records on and we had a great night. I was going to the Milk Cup.

CHAPTER 13

Mark, The New Saturday Boy

All week I was worried about what was I going to tell Nigel, and that I couldn't help him on the run. I thought I could just pull a sicky but what if he found out? I asked my mum what to do and she said, "Just be honest, son. He will understand."

So Saturday morning I got up at the usual time and headed down to Dover Street to meet Nigel. As I walked down the Shankill all I could think of was the county team and who we would be playing against; what if I got noticed by a scout and even got a trial for one of the big teams? As I turned into Dover Street, there was Nigel, parked as usual in his big red lorry. I walked over and opened the passenger door. I took a deep breath but when I lifted my head to explain to Nigel, who was this sitting in the lorry with him? *Another boy? What the fuck?* I thought.

Nigel looked at me. "Jonny, this is my son, Mark.

He is going to help on a Saturday as well."

Mark looked round – he was a couple of years younger than me, with short dark hair. I didn't know what to say.

"What's wrong, Jonny? Cat got your tongue?" Nigel asked.

"I can't go today, Nigel. I got selected for the county football team and I have to go and meet the manger this morning. I'm really sorry for letting you down but I will be here next week."

"Don't worry, son. That's brilliant news. Sure, I will see you here next Saturday, same time," Nigel replied.

As I closed the door, Nigel drove off to start the run. *My run, my job,* I thought.

As I walked back up the Shankill I was raging. *Nigel has brought his son out to replace me. What am I going to do? Have I just been sacked? I needed that job, I needed the money.*

Just at that, Stevo was walking down the road.

"Alright Jonny, not working the day?" he asked.

"No mate, I have to go and meet the manager of the county team and pay my money to get registered to play," I replied.

"Brilliant mate, it's great you got picked. Remember your mates when you're earn'n the big bucks," Stevo said.

"Aye mate, will do," I laughed.

As I walked on I couldn't get Mark out of my head. *He's getting my tips today and probably getting my job.*

I walked through the front door and my mum had breakfast on the table. I sat down.

"Mum, Nigel has his son out working with him now," I said as I took a gulp of tea.

"Oh, and what's the problem?" she asked.

"What if he doesn't need me anymore and I don't have a job?"

"Nigel wouldn't do that, son. Stop worrying. Come on now, eat up, you have to go and get to the Dub to meet Mr Spence."

I looked up at the clock and it read ten past nine. S*hit, I had better go. I have to meet Gerrerd.*

I threw on my coat; my mum gave me the other thirty quid. I was just about to go out the door when she called me.

"Jonny, hold on. You need your birth certificate." She reached down behind the sofa and pulled out an old briefcase. She opened it up and plundered through it and gave me a sheet of paper – it was my birth certificate.

"Hold on to that and don't lose it, and here, there is five pound as well for the bus, and get yourself something to eat for lunch."

She gave me a big hug and out the door I went.

As I got to the top of Tennett Street I was hoping Gerrerd was there. Yes! I waved over. Gerrerd was sitting on the wall; he waved back.

"Alright mate, you got the money then?" I asked.

"Aye mate, don't know where my ma got it from and I really don't want to know," he replied.

We started walking down the Crumlin Road; Gerrerd flagged down a black taxi and we both got in.

"Into town mate," Gerrerd said.

The taxi driver turned round and guess what? It was the big fat man who usually works the Shankill.

"Alright Jonny lad, where you two lads going the day?" he asked.

I stuttered and stammered, "We, we have to, to go to the, the Dub. We both made, made the, the county team and, and we, we have to, to get, get registered."

Gerrerd looked at me like I had two heads.

"Have you taken a stupid pill, Jonny? You're talking like an edgit."

The taxi man said, "To the Dub? Is that over near Taughmonagh?"

"It is, mister," Gerrerd replied.

I just looked at Gerrerd; my face was a pure render.

"You feeling alright, Jonny?" Gerrerd asked.

"Aye mate, just a bit warm." My mind was doing overtime. What if the taxi man said anything to my ma? She would want to know who Gerrerd was and my da would kill me for hanging about with a lad from Ardoyne.

The taxi man said, "Well Jonny, things are looking good for me. I still have your signature and you're in the counties. Hit the big time son, I will run the both of you over and back if your mate gives me his signature."

Gerrerd's eyes lit up. "Aye mister, no problem. Anything for a free lift."

The taxi man reached into the glove compartment and pulled out a pen and paper. Gerrerd signed his name ('Thanks for the lift – Gerrerd Kelly').

The taxi man thanked him and off we went to the Dub. It took about fifteen minutes but it was the longest fifteen minutes ever.

When we arrived there were a lot of parents and the rest of the squad. All the players were asked to go into one of the function rooms where we had to pay the fifty quid and give over our birth certificates.

Each player in turn was handed a kit bag with our initials on. *Wow,* I thought. *My name on a bag.* When I opened it, inside was full training gear, a tracksuit, and a jacket. Oh my god, this was brilliant. Even better that, our initials was on each piece of gear – we had really hit the big time.

Mr Spence gave us an envelope and explained the training dates and times, and he also explained what was expected of us on and off the pitch, and that we were representing County Antrim. Any bad behaviour would not be tolerated.

Me and Gerrerd got a lift back into town and got off at City Hall. We gave the taxi man two quid each and thanked him for taking us.

As we stood there in Belfast we were both beaming with joy at getting signed up for County Antrim, and stood looking at City Hall. Gerrerd turned to me. "We have to go for a fry-up, mate, to celebrate."

"You're right, mate. Where will we go?" I asked.

"I know a wee place not too far from here."

Five minutes' walk and we were in a wee side street café. As we walked through the door the girl turned round.

"Alright Gerrerd. How's you, son?" she asked.

"Dead on, Rosie. How's the form with you?"

"Yeah, ok love. What would you and your mate like?" she asked.

"We are celebrating. Two of your big frys and two teas."

"What's the big occasion?" she asked.

"We both made the county football team and we are on the road to stardom." Gerrerd laughed when he said that.

"Is your mate alright or has he lost his tongue?" the girl asked.

I had just realised I hadn't said a word. "No missus, just quiet."

"That's super, boys. Grab yourselves a pew and I will bring your fry-ups over."

We sat down by the window and had a good look at our gear. It was black and yellow, really class-looking, but what set it off was our initials embroidered into it.

"That's class, Gerrerd, isn't it?" I said.

"Aye mate, really brill," he replied as he looked at the tracksuit top. Just at that, Rosie came over with two plates of the biggest fry-up I had ever seen.

Two soda, two potato, two eggs, two bacon, two sausages, mushrooms, tomatoes, and even some chips. I said to Gerrerd, "Holy shit, mate. I don't know whether to climb this or eat it."

"Get it into, Jonny. It will put meat on them tin ribs of yours."

We must have sat there for thirty minutes, eating. Every mouthful was beaut and washed down with a big mug of tea, and all for 1.50 each. You couldn't beat it with a big stick.

As we dandered back up Crumlin Road Gerrerd did most of the talking, telling me that he had two older brothers and a younger sister. He said that his dad worked for a parcel delivery company and he went as far as Coleraine and Ballyclare and worked late most days. I told Gerrerd that I had no brothers and sisters and my mum and dad didn't work, but we were happy, and that we had lived in Broom Street all my life. He told me that he used to live over of the Falls road but they moved as they needed a bigger house, so they had been living in Ardoyne for about ten years now. He didn't like living there as their house was behind the shops at Ardoyne and it got really rough at times, especially in July when the marching season was at its peak.

As we walked past the Crumlin Road jail, Gerrerd said, "I remember one night, it was a Saturday, and a lot of my mates had got together to start a fight with the police. It was about 9 o'clock at night and it really got out of hand. The I.R.A. got involved and shots were fired. It was terrible and two days after that there was about ten houses raided and eight people were arrested and charged with riotous behaviour. My two older brothers were lifted as well but they weren't charged. My da beat the crap out of them for even being there. It was terrible mate, if we could get out of there we would. I absolutely hate living there, it's the same awl crap and the I.R.A. would shoot you if you said anything. What's round your way like?"

"Not as bad as that, Gerrerd, but then our wee street isn't anywhere near the peace line so it's just the same faces, and the only trouble is when the bars get out and the headers with too much drink decide to fight. It's good crack to watch but I couldn't stick what you put up with, it must be terrible."

"Aye mate, that's why I want to make it as a footballer. It's my way out, and as soon as I get a contract, I'm away. Even better if it's across the water, the further from this shit hole the better."

As we got to Tennett Street I said, "That's me, mate. What you up to later?"

"Nothing, probably just sit in. There isn't much to do round our way. What you up to?"

"Same, maybe head up to the Woodvale to see if any of my mates are playing a match."

"Sounds good. I would come down but I know how it is. Do you fancy meeting me tomorrow and we will go into town for a dander?"

"Aye, Gerrerd, that would be great. What time?"

"Bout one, mate, if that suits you. I have to go to Mass first but I will be out for twelve so by the time I get home and get changed, I will meet you here for one."

"Mass? What's that?" I asked.

"Church. My ma makes me go. I frig'n hate it but it's easier to go and keep her happy."

"Dead on, see you at one then," and I walked off down Tennett Street.

Just at that, Nigel pulled out onto Tennett Street and parked outside a row of houses. I walked up to the van just as he got out.

"Alright Nigel, how yous going?"

"Awk Jonny, alright son. Aye, going ok. Did you get to your football?"

"Aye Nigel, got this bag of gear as well," I replied as I showed it to him. Mark got out of the van and went to do a call. He smiled over at me and I said, "Alright Mark, you steeling my tips today?"

He turned round.

"Aye, Jonny," and he laughed as he knocked the door of his call.

Nigel said, "Don't listen to him, he's winding you up, Jonny."

I gave a forced laugh and said, "Oh right, Nigel I will see you next Saturday," and I walked off.

I was raging. That fucker had stolen my job, and what was I going to do? I needed it.

I got home and just went straight up to my room.

As I lay there on my bed I thought about Gerrerd and him living in Ardoyne, and what he had to put up with. He was dead on and I was looking forward to meeting him the next day.

My mum came in.

"Well Jonny, how'd you get on?"

"Brilliant, Ma. Look what I got." I opened the kit bag and lifted out the gear.

"Put it on you, son, and come down and show me."

She went downstairs and I put the tracksuit on. As I stood there in my room looking at my reflection in the mirror, I thought to myself, *I'm a county player*, and as I looked up at Norman Whiteside's photo, I said, "I'm going to play for Man U someday, you just wait and see, Norman."

I turned and went downstairs. My mum stood there in the living room; she was smiling from ear to ear.

"Awk Jonny, look at you, you're a real handsome lad. Come here, I'll fix you." She fixed the collar of my top. "That's better, now away down to the bar and show your da."

"What, Ma? Go to the Mountain View?"

"Yes son, and bring your da home with you."

Out the door I went and I walked down the street and into the Mountain View bar. As I walked through the front door it was packed and I couldn't see my da. I asked the girl behind the bar, "Have you seen my da, Jimmy Andrews?"

"Aye son, he's out the back. I will get him for you."

As I stood there in the bar I could feel a thousand eyes staring at me. Just at that, my da came in.

"Oh my god, Jonny I hardly recognised you there

in your new gear. Let me see you."

I was scundered; everyone was staring and to make it worse my da said, "This here is my son Jonny, and he's going to play for Linfield someday."

The whole bloody bar cheered. My face was a pure redner. "Da, we have to go. My ma's got the dinner out."

"Tell your ma I'll be home in a bit."

I couldn't get out of the bar quick enough – I was scundered. I walked back up home and me and my ma had our dinner together. It must have been after ten before my da came home, blind drunk as usual.

CHAPTER 14

The Robbery

Gerrerd and I became very good friends; we met most Sundays and at county training. We had become very close, even though we came from different communities we had so much in common.

The following Saturday I turned up to meet Nigel and his son, Mark, and to be honest Mark was dead on. He was a bit younger than me but had a bit of crack about him.

When we came into the street that the cat woman lived in I looked at Nigel. "Nigel, we should let Mark do the next call. The woman has a couple of cats and she always gives you a tip."

"Good idea, Jonny. Our Mark would love that, they are really lovely cats," Nigel replied.

Mark got out of the van. I shouted out the window, "Just take four mixed in, Mark. Just rap the door and go on in but make sure you close the door behind you in case the cats get out."

As Mark lifted the lemonade and went on into the smelly cat woman's house, Nigel and I were in stitches.

"You're a bad egg, Jonny," Nigel said, laughing.

"You got me, Nigel, so only fair I return the favour."

Just at that, Mark came back out of the house, put the empty bottles into a crate and got into the van. Me and Nigel were stunned – he wasn't even coughing.

"You alright Mark? Did you see the cats?" I asked.

"Aye mate, she has got about ten cats in there but she's a really nice wee woman, gave me 50p tip as well."

I just looked over at Nigel, who shrugged his shoulders.

"Was the house ok, Mark? Any smell?" I asked.

"Mate, I have no sense of smell so I wouldn't know."

I burst out laughing.

"You're a lucky man, Mark. When I have to do that house I need a gas mask, so from now on it's your call."

"Spot on, Jonny. 50p tip every week, not a problem."

The three of us had a quare laugh about it.

A few weeks passed and it was when we were sitting eating our chips in Conway Street in Nigel's van that both doors were pulled open.

"Give us the money you aul bastard or you're gonna get shot."

My heart was thumping; two lads were standing at Nigel's door, both wearing baseball caps and scarfs over their faces. One of them had his hand in his pocket, pointing at Nigel when he said he was going to shoot him. Another lad was standing at my door; he grabbed me by my top.

"Give us the money, ballbag."

I looked hard at him. I fucking knew him – it was Jonty who had bullied me in school – and when I turned and looked at the other two, they were his two henchmen, Paul and Jason.

They repeated it.

"Give us the money or else."

"Or else what?" Nigel said, as he jumped out of the van. Before I knew it Nigel had lifted a baton from behind his seat and whacked Jason across the head.

"You wee fuckers, I'll smash your heads in," Nigel said as he laid into both of them.

The squeals from both of them were deafening. *Whack, whack, whack*, as Nigel really gave them both a pasting.

Meanwhile, at my side of the van Jonty didn't know what to do. He threw my chips in the air and ran off down the street. Jason and Paul weren't too far behind him but they weren't out of trouble yet. I had never seen Nigel move as fast in my life; he sprinted down the street after the three of them, shouting, "I'll break your legs, you wee fuckers, if you ever come near me again."

When Nigel came back up to the van me and Mark were stunned. We both sat there in silence after what had just happened.

"Yous ok, boys? Did any of you get hit?"

We both turned to face Nigel.

"Dad, I think I've pissed myself." Mark started crying.

"It's ok, son, they're away. We will get you sorted. Stop crying, you're ok."

Nigel looked over at me.

"Jonny, you ok?"

"No, Nigel. My fuck'n chips are all over the floor."

Nigel started laughing. "Your chips? Is that all?"

I was gutted. I was really enjoying those chips.

We drove up to my house and I brought Mark in to get changed. There was nobody in so no questions to answer. When we both got back into the van I said to Nigel, "Don't be saying anything to my ma, Nigel. She wouldn't let me come back out again if she knew we nearly got robbed."

"No problem, son. Mum's the word."

Near the end of the run two men approached the van. Nigel got out.

"Can I help you, lads?" Nigel said as he put his hand behind his seat.

Shit, here we go again, I thought. I looked at Mark and he really looked frightened.

"Are you Nigel?" one of the men asked.

"Yes I am. What's wrong?" Nigel asked.

"Calm down, Nigel, We are from the U.V.F. I

believe you had a bit of bother earlier."

"Yeah, I did. Three lads tried to rob me."

"We know all about it. We won't accept that sort of behaviour on our road. You can be sure we will be looking into it, we are just here to tell you that you won't be touched. This type of behaviour will be dealt with. Do you know who the lads were?"

My heart was thumping. I knew the three of them but I daren't say a word, I just put my head down.

"No, the lads were all wearing scarfs over their faces so no, I don't know them."

"No worries. They won't do it again once we get the hold of them."

Nigel thanked them and the two men walked off. Nigel got into the van.

"Well that's them sorted. I wouldn't like to be in their shoes now."

"No Nigel, neither would I."

I didn't go out the rest of the night. I was too scared in case I ran into Jonty and his mates.

CHAPTER 15

The Milk Cup

In the run-up to the Milk Cup, Gerrerd and I travelled to and from training and to our warm-up games. We were now best mates, meeting most Saturday nights and Sundays. I didn't hang around with Stevo anymore as he was now working and had other mates.

July rolled round and it was time to play at the Milk Cup.

We travelled up in a coach and we were staying in a hostel in Coleraine where it was two to a room, so me and Gerrerd stayed together. The opening ceremony was superb, all the teams that were competing walked through the town and it was the Manchester United team that caught my eye – they were giants and everyone was in awe of them. They were superb-looking in their red tracksuits. The whole talk was that this squad was the future first team, and especially four of the team – Ryan Giggs, a wiry winger with loads of ability and pace to burn; Nicky Butt, a hard midfield player with bright ginger hair; another ginger-haired player, Paul Scholes, he wasn't as tall as the other players but would kick you just for fun; and an upcoming star called David Beckham. Looking at him, I said to Gerrerd, "There's your man, David Beckham. They say he's going to be the best player in the world someday."

"Aye right, look at him. He looks like a fruit with his hair in curtains. I would kick lumps out of him," Gerrerd replied.

"Just as well we aren't playing against them. They are in the premier section, we would have to win our group to have any chance of getting a game with them." I said that with a lot of hope. Imagine playing against the so-called next Man U first team, now that would be a dream come true.

The next morning we all went for breakfast – porridge and toast – then off for a training session, which was quite light, just a bit of ball work and some stretching. Then we went for lunch, where we talked about our first game which was a 3pm kick-off against a team from Turkey called Feyenord. Also in our group were Russia, Motherwell, and Crewe Alexandra, so it was a tough group to try and qualify from, but the lads were buzzing to get started.

We travelled to the ground at 1.30 and took a walk round the pitch, eyeballing the Feyenord team. Gerrerd said to me, "Them boys look tough, don't they Jonny?"

"Aye mate, but we will just have to get stuck in.

We want to get off to a good start."

We were all called in to get changed; it was now just after 2pm, fifty minutes to kick-off.

We were again well-stretched by Mr Spence and the two coaches, and over the space of about twenty minutes Mr Spence spoke to each of the lads. When it was my turn he called me over.

"You ok Jonny? Don't be worrying about this game, the Turkish lads should fear us. We just have to stick to the game plan and we will be fine. Have you any wee niggles needs looked at, son?"

"No Mr Spence, just raring to go."

"That's what I like to hear. For the first twenty minutes have a go at their left back, see if you can get to the byline and put a few crosses in, but after the third go, take him on the inside and go direct yourself. Don't be afraid to shoot, son, 'cause you're a talented wee lad and you will frighten the life out of this team."

"I will, Mr Spence." Any nerves I had were gone, I just couldn't wait to get the game started.

2.40pm and we went back into the changing rooms to get changed into our playing kit. The team was named and the last instructions given, and we were off.

As we walked onto the pitch we were greeted with a huge round of applause from the crowd of about 300. The atmosphere was super as I stood there on right wing. I looked at the left back and thought, *You're mine today, son. This is my turn to shine.*

The ref blew his whistle and off we went. We had

kick-off so the ball was passed back to our right back, who immediately launched it forward and I was off running. The left back took a bad touch and I flicked the ball past him and to the byline I went. I whipped a cross in to be met by our centre forward, who put it over the bar. The crowd clapped and I got back into position.

The game went back and forward with both teams wanting to win and get off to a good start. Feyenord came very close on a couple of occasions with two goal line clearances from Gerrerd to keep them out, but it was on the stroke of half time when the deadlock was broken. Feyenord had a corner and we all marked up, but it was their big captain who met the ball and headed home; 1-0 down and the half time whistle went.

When we got back into the changing rooms Mr Spence told us we were playing superb, just got caught ball watching on a couple of occasions, but we were holding our own and had to keep attacking the full backs.

"Jonny, you move over to the left wing. I want you to cut inside and have a go. If we don't get at them then we will struggle defensively as they will cut us apart on the counter attack."

"Ok Mr Spence, I will do my best."

When we went back out onto the pitch all the lads were buzzing. We knew we were in with a chance. I said to Gerrerd, "Mate, just keep a high line. We have to play in their half if we have any chance of scoring."

"Will do, Jonny. Let's do this."

The ref blew his whistle and the second half

began. The Feyenord team played really deep and just tried to hold onto possession, but against our team – no chance. The left back got the ball and I was on him like a rash. I nicked the ball off him and cut inside. The centre half lunged into a challenge but I flicked the ball over him and I was through on goal. I saw the keeper come off his line to close me down and I dropped my shoulder and sold him the dumby. I rolled the ball into the open net and we were back on level terms – one each.

Chance after chance we had, but just couldn't finish. The game ended one each and we both got a point.

The next four days saw us play Russia, which we won 2-1. I got an assist. Then we played Motherwell – they were superb. They beat us 2-0. Our last game was against Crewe Alexandre. We had to at least get a draw out of this one to try and qualify as runners up, as Motherwell hadn't lost a game – they were group winners so it was between us and Crewe for second place. They needed to win but we just needed a draw.

Ninety minutes of football and we couldn't be separated – 0-0 and it looked like we had done it until Gerrerd mistimed a challenge and the ref blew for a penalty.

My heart sunk; we were going out. I was the only player left out on the right wing. I couldn't bear to watch as the captain of Crewe struck the ball from twelve yards. The crowd cheered. As I turned I saw every player run up the pitch towards me. *What the fuck?* I thought. As I looked up the ball dropped beside me and I heard Gerrerd shout, "Go Jonny! Go!"

I picked the ball up in my own half and I have never run as fast in my life. Only the keeper to beat. Forty yards... thirty yards... twenty yards... and the keeper came rushing out. I chipped it over him and scored. The crowd went mad and my teammates all dove on me. We won 1-0 and qualified for the knockout stages.

That night back at the dorms we were given pizzas for dinner to celebrate, and everyone was in good form. The crack was brilliant; we could hardly sleep at the excitement at getting to the knockout stage.

The next evening we were to play Leeds United, another top club from England, and unfortunately we didn't win. We lost 1-0 and were knocked out, but the week we had there was superb and to qualify from the group we were in was a real success, and everyone knew it.

We watched the final, which was Man U against Leeds, and wow, what a game. Extra time and penalties to decide the winner and David Beckham stood up and scored the winner, so Man U won 5-4 on pens and were crowned champions.

CHAPTER 16

A Dark Day On The Shankill

After the Milk Cup I was asked to go for trials with a number of clubs, but I had to wait until I had turned sixteen, which was in August, so it was a really exciting time. I couldn't believe when Linfield came knocking at my door. It was the 16th of October. I had just finished work with Nigel when a big car pulled up outside my house. Mr Spence got out with another fella and came to the door.

"Hello Mrs Andrews, I am Brian Adair. I am head of recruitment at Linfield. Could we have ten minutes of your time?"

My mum and I were speechless but she brought them in and we all sat down.

"How can I help you, Mr Adair?" she asked.

Mr Spence said, "I have been following your Jonny for a while now, but his performances in the Milk Cup have stirred up quite an interest and a number of clubs have made inquiries about him, but we at Linfield would love for him to come and play for us, and that's why we are here. As I said, this is Mr Adair. He will answer any questions you have."

I sat there on our sofa in our wee house, just in shock. *Linfield wants me – wee Jonny from the Shankill.*

My mum said, "What, do you mean Linfield youth team wants Jonny?"

"No, Mrs Andrews. We think Jonny could be a first team player even at sixteen. He could play a part for us and cement down a first team place, but it won't be easy. He's going to have to work hard. We train three times a week and then a match on a Saturday, but we would be offering him thirty quid a week starting off, and then with appearances that could go up."

"That sounds all well and good but is he not too young? He's only sixteen."

"No, Mrs Andrews. If you're good enough, you're definitely old enough, and again we will look after Jonny. It will be a good move for him as we feel it's about his future, and we would love to be part of his progress. This is only the start for Jonny – he is quite capable of going a lot further."

"What do you think, Jonny?" my mum asked.

"I would love to sign for Linfield, Mum."

"Right, it's settled then. What happens now, Mr Adair?"

"Well next Saturday we play Glentoran at Windsor. We would like Jonny to come up and watch the game, and then afterwards meet the manager and put pen to paper."

"That sounds great. What time do you need him there for?"

"Well it's a 5pm kick-off so if Jonny is up for about four that would be perfect. I will meet him at the players' entrance."

"Brilliant, he will be there."

Mr Spence and Mr Adair shook my hand and my mum's. They thanked me and said they would see me next Saturday.

When they left, me and my mum sat down. My mum threw her arms round me.

"Jonny, you're going to be a Linfield player. You're on your way to stardom, son. I'm so pleased for you, son. Wait till your da hears, he's going to be over the moon. His wee Jonny, playing for Linfield."

"Aye, Ma. I can't believe it."

Just at that, my da came through the front door.

"Jimmy! Jimmy, our Jonny's going to sign for Linfield. Two men from Windsor are just away, they want him to sign next Saturday. He's going to be a star."

"What? Annie, what do you mean?"

My mum was standing crying; I stood up.

"My ma's right, Da. I'm signing next Saturday after the Glentoran game. They are paying me thirty quid a week starting off and once I break into the first team it will go up."

My da threw his arms round me, lifted me up, and

spun me round.

"Super, son. I'm chuffed to bits for you. This calls for a celebration. Annie, get the good plates out and get the teapot on."

My da reached into his pocket and pulled out a fiver. "Here, Jonny. Away down to the chippy and get three fish suppers; we are having a party."

As I walked down the street I felt ten foot high. Me, the Linfield player. I was miles away dreaming about playing for them and playing in front of hundreds of people at Windsor. I didn't even hear the girl in the chippy ask me for my order. It was only when Jonty hit me with a punch on the arm that I came back to earth.

"Alright ballbag," he said.

My arm was throbbing. "Alright Jonty," I replied.

"What you at, Jonny?" he asked.

"Nothing Jonty, just getting the dinner in for my ma and da."

I wasn't telling him anything. He wouldn't have believed me anyway; he was turning out to be a real hard ticket. Him, Paul, and Jason were getting a reputation on the road and the U.D.A. were looking after them so nobody would mess with them, 'cause if you did you would be on the end of a beating.

"Oh right, ballbag, a wee night in with the parents. I'm off to Heather Street, there is a charity do on the night. Should be good crack if you fancy it, mate. We would spot you a couple of drinks."

"No, Jonty. I'm alright, I got to get going."

Just at that, the girl behind the counter gave me my fish and chips.

"Watch you don't drop them ones," Jonty said, laughing.

I knew what he meant when he said that. What I should have said was, 'Aye, and watch Nigel doesn't hit you again round the head with his baton,' but what I did say was, "Aye mate, I will hold these ones tight."

And I walked out of the chippy and up home.

That night when I went to bed I was so excited I couldn't sleep a wink. I got up the next morning absolutely shattered, so Sunday was a day in and a bit of TV. In fact, all week was the same. I couldn't put the week in quick enough.

It was Saturday and I had to give Nigel the bad news that I couldn't work for him anymore. After we got the run finished he pulled up to my door.

"Nigel, I have some bad news to tell you."

"What is it, Jonny?" he replied.

"I have to give up working for you. I have been asked to go and sign for Linfield and I won't be able to make Saturdays anymore. I hope you understand."

"Jonny, you're a footballer, son. You have to go with your dreams, and don't worry, our Mark can do the run now. I wondered why you were so quiet today."

Nigel got out of the van and came round to my side. He gave me a hug and wished me all the best.

As Nigel's van pulled away from my house, I thought about all the good times I had out on the run and was a bit sad at that chapter of my life now being over.

But a new chapter was about to begin. Into the house I went and up to get changed. It was 12.30 and I had to be over at Windsor for three. I was that excited I got changed in a flash. I put on my Milk Cup tracksuit and downstairs I went. My mum was standing in the living room.

"Oh look at you, you're all grown up looking. Come here and give your mum a hug before you go."

I walked over and gave my mum a hug; she squeezed me really tight.

"I'm so proud of you, Jonny. Go and get your dream, son."

Out the door I went and started walking down the Shankill. I was absolutely buzzing; I was walking on air; I felt like a real superstar. I stopped outside the pawn shop – a ring had caught my eye as I stood there looking in the window at the most gorgeous ring I had ever seen. It was a Rangers gold sovereign ring and I said to myself, *I'm gonna buy you, son, when I get my first month's wages.* It was priced at sixty quid but I told myself, *You're worth it, son.* I turned to walk on down the road and just at that, two men in overalls pushed past me. One of them was carrying a grip bag and I shouted after them, "Here, take your time, lads. You near knocked me over."

One of the men turned round and just gave me a real dirty look. They both walked into Frizzell's fish shop. As I walked past one of the men ran past me. There was a lot of screaming inside the shop and just as I turned to see what was happening there was a huge bang and I was blown onto the road.

As I lay there on the Shankill road the ringing in my ears was Deafening. I couldn't move, I couldn't breathe; the dust from the bricks was all over me. I passed out for a while; when I came round I heard a man's voice.

"Son, can you hear me? Son, can you hear me?"

I nodded my head. He was lifting bricks off me; I was still struggling to breathe. The dust was up my nose and in my eyes, the taste of dirt in my mouth, and then the pain started. My legs were still buried in the rubble but the pain travelled up my body. I coughed and coughed. I heard the man shout, "Somebody help me! This lad's alive! Somebody get a car quick, he is losing blood. Get a fucking car! He needs the hospital!"

I had passed out again and when I came round I was in the back of a black taxi driving really fast down the road. The man was in the back of the cab with me; he was holding a coat onto one of my legs really tightly.

"You will be ok, son. We are going to the Mater Hospital, you will be there soon, just hold on."

"What happened, mister? Was it a bomb?"

"Yes son, it was a bomb. You're lucky to be alive, now just hold on, we are nearly there."

Just at that, the cab screeched to a halt and the doors were flung open. Hospital staff lifted me out of the cab and onto a bed; they wheeled me into the hospital and started working on me.

That day on the Shankill the I.R.A. walked into

Frizzell's fish shop and planted a bomb. It went off prematurely and killed ten people, one of them being the bomber Thomas Begley.

Fifty-seven other people were injured and I was one of them.

That dark day on the Shankill changed my life forever.

CHAPTER 17

A New Start And A New Job

I spent a long time in hospital. They thought at first I would lose my right leg but after numerous operations they saved it. My mum and dad visited me every day and Gerrerd came as well a few times. It was a long period of time – hard time – and it was about three months later when I started physio, and that was the worst time of my life. I had to learn to walk again as after the operations I had and the length of time I had spent in a hospital bed, my muscles had wasted away. I knew the first day of trying to stand that I would never kick a ball again, and that ripped the heart out of me, my dreams taken away from me, but my mum and dad kept reminding me that I was lucky to be alive. But sometimes, lying in bed at night, I wished I had been killed 'cause my life was football, and after leaving school with no qualifications my chances of a job were slim.

Weeks passed and every day I got a little bit

stronger. It was six months in total that I had spent in hospital but the day came that I was released and sent home.

It was a Friday afternoon and we got a taxi up home. When we got in my mum said, "Go up and get changed, son. We are going out."

"Where are we going, Mum?" I asked.

"Never mind, just go and get changed."

I went up the stairs and put a pair of jeans on and a jumper; I was wondering where we were going and when I came back downstairs my mum and dad were standing in the open door.

"Right, let's go," my dad said.

We walked down Broom Street and turned left; we walked for about five minutes.

"Where are we going, Ma?" I asked.

"Never you mind, we are here," she replied.

We were standing outside Heather Street Social Club and the man at the door said, "Hello Jonny, how are you son?"

"Alright mister, but don't know what I'm doing here."

"Go on in, son. You will find out when you go in."

The man opened the door and a huge cheer went up as I walked in. The music started playing as well; it scared the crap out of me. Everyone was there – the neighbours, my mates from football, even Nigel and his wife Dorothy were there. It was brilliant, like all my Christmases rolled into one.

I turned and gave my mum and dad a big hug and thanked them. It was brilliant – a real welcome home.

That night the man behind the bar introduced himself.

"Hello Jonny, my name is Billy Lock. I run the bar and I was wondering what you're doing for work."

"Nothing Billy, I haven't got a job."

"That's lucky for me then, 'cause I'm looking for someone to help behind the bar. Would you be interested? It's full-time."

I didn't know what to say. This day couldn't get any better.

"Yes Billy, I would love to work for you."

"Then it's settled, you're my new barman. You start Monday – we open up at 6pm so I will see you then."

Brilliant, I thought. Things were looking up.

My mum grabbed my arm.

"Come on you, come and dance with your wee mum."

Oh my god, I was scundered. Me up dancing with my ma, and to make it worse my da staggered over and started dancing with us too. It was a train wreck, me getting burled round by my ma and all my mates standing laughing their heads off. My da then decided he was going to sing with the band and guess what? Bloody Kenny Rodgers and The Gambler. That was my cue to get off side, and into the back room I went.

As I walked in there was a table of men sitting talking. I didn't know any of them but one of them looked over.

"Alright son, glad to see you're on your feet again. I believe we are having you as our new barman."

"Yes mister, I start on Monday."

"My name is Norman, this is Jock, Billy, Joe, Sam, and Phil. If you need anything, and I mean anything, come and see any of us. We will look after you from now on."

The blood ran from me. Goose bumps were all over me. It hit me – this is the U.D.A. and this is their meeting place.

"Ok Norman, I will remember that."

Back out the door I went. I would rather be up dancing with my ma and listening to my da sing than be in the same room as those men. They were killers and if you ever crossed them you would end up in a skip.

*

Monday night and my first shift in the bar. When I walked into the bar, Billy was already there.

"Alright Jonny, are you ready to join the workers?"

"Yes Billy, what needs done?"

"You need to light the fire first to get a bit of heat in this place. The coal and sticks are in the store room." Billy pointed over to a door in the corner of the room.

Two goes it took to get the fire lit, and I was bloody stinking. I went into the toilets to wash my hands and as I stood there washing them I looked round; the place was stinking. I thought to myself, *This place needs a good clean. You'd be better pissing out in the yard than pissing here. You'd catch something in this toilet.*

I went out into the bar. "Billy, what else needs done?"

"We need to bottle up. Can you see what's needed behind the bar?"

I lifted a pen and paper from behind the bar and made a list of what was needed.

"Where are the bottles of beer, Billy?"

"Come on and I will show you where the store room is, son."

We walked into another room behind the bar. It was dimly lit and there were kegs of beer with pipes running everywhere, then over in the corner was a rack with cases of drink and tins of Coke on it.

"Just lift what's needed, Jonny, and fill the fridges. We have a darts team in tonight and they usually drink quite a bit. Come over here and I will show you how to change a barrel."

After stocking the shelves and a bit of a tidy up, we were ready to open up.

That night was a darts match and a local derby game, so there was a good crowd in and I was kept busy all night. I didn't realise how much some people could drink; the women were worse than the men – they could put the drink away rightly.

This one girl was as wide as she was tall and she sat at the bar all night. Her name was Lilly and she introduced herself as Orange Lil, and her husband was her wee Victor. He was a slim build of a man and was very quiet. I thought to myself, *What the hell does Victor see in Lilly? And to marry her, he has got a heart like a lion.*

All night Orange Lil drank vodka and Diet Coke, and tortured the life out of me. She said to me, "What's your name good looking?"

"Jonny, I only started tonight."

"It's about time Billy brought some talent to work here."

My face was a pure redner. I didn't know what to say.

"Do you want a wee drink, Jonny?"

"No Lilly, I'm fine," I replied as I poured her another vodka.

She handed me a tenner.

"Take one for yourself, good looking."

As I turned to ring the money into the till I heard her say, "Oh, look at the arse on you. You're a fine specimen of a man. What age are you, son?"

My face was beaming. Billy overheard her as well.

"Never you mind, Lilly," he said. "He's too young for you, you would gobble him up."

I just stood there totally scundered; I was stuck for words.

"Now there is a thought, Billy, Gobbling Jonny up."

She lifted her drink and downed it in one.

"Set them up again, Jonny, and this time you may get my Victor a pint as well."

I looked at Victor; he just stood there, silent. I thought to myself, *I'm sure he's glad she is torturing me and leaving him alone.*

A big cheer went up and the Heather Street darts team had won against the Mountain View, so all was good.

It was about 1am when we finally got the last person out and got the glasses lifted. Billy said to me, "Did you enjoy that, son? You worked hard tonight."

"I did, Billy. It was good crack. Your woman Orange Lil is a handful, isn't she?"

"Aye Jonny, she is hard work, just don't get caught on your own with her. She would tie you down and you would be done with." He stood there laughing.

"Why do you call her Orange Lil?" I asked.

"Awk Jonny, look at her bake. She has more makeup on than Boots Chemist has on their shelves, and to be honest she needs it. She's not blessed with good looks. I feel sorry for Victor – when she gets the drink in she beats the head of him and God love him, he just loves her."

As Billy pulled the shutter down to lock it we both stood there laughing.

"Do you want a lift home, son?" Billy asked.

"No Billy, I only live up the street."

"I know Jonny, but these are dark days we are living in. There is a lot of tit for tat killings going on and I don't want you walking home on your own. You never know who is out prowling the streets at this hour."

"Ok Billy, I will take a lift then."

Literally two minutes in the car and I was outside my front door. I got out and thanked Billy for giving me the job and the lift. He replied, "See you tomorrow night, son. Same time. It's a pool match so be roughly the same sort of numbers."

"Ok Billy, see you then."

And into the house I went; my ma had tea and toast ready for me.

"There's the worker. Now how'd you get on, son?"

"Aye Ma, it was good. I really enjoyed it. Some headers live on the Shankill, you get a quare laugh with them."

"That's good, son. As long as you enjoyed it."

I ate my toast and drank my tea, and went on up to bed. I was shattered.

My life went on like that, working in the bar at nights and meeting Gerrerd whenever I could, but we slowly drifted apart and I never really saw him anymore.

*

A year or so went past and it was one Thursday night Billy asked me to stay on a bit as there was a committee meeting, and we closed the bar early that evening, 10 o'clock, to be precise.

I tidied up and washed the glasses. As I was standing behind the bar all these men started coming in and sat down round four tables that Billy had set out.

Billy called over to me, "Jonny, take a drinks order for these men."

I lifted a pen and piece of paper and went round each one and took their orders. They were tough-looking boys. There were ten of them altogether and it looked very serious.

As I stood behind the bar pouring the drinks, Billy walked over in front of me.

"Jonny, when I said this is a committee meeting I should of told you this is the U.F.F. and they are here to sort out some business. So whatever you see or hear doesn't leave this room. You have been working here long enough now to understand how to keep your mouth shut."

"Yes Billy, you have no need to worry. I won't say a word."

I just kept pouring the drinks all night; these men were the bosses who made the decisions on everything that the U.F.F. did and I heard a lot of things that night – names being mentioned, who was to get pulled in and kneecapped, what money was to be brought in and paid out. It was a case of hear no evil, speak no evil. I was petrified by what was talked about, and to make it worse I was now part of it.

I poured drinks many a night for those committee meetings and was now on first-name terms with all who attended, but it was one late Thursday night after one of the meetings that a guy called Joe asked me stay behind when all the other men had left.

"Jonny lad, can you stay on a while? I need to speak with Billy for five minutes."

I lifted my head from behind the bar; I looked at Billy and said, "Aye Joe, that's fine."

It was about ten minutes later when Billy came over to me; he handed me the keys to the shutter.

"Jonny, you lock up tonight. I will see you as normal tomorrow night."

And Billy left.

"Jonny, sit down, son. I have something to ask you."

I was really nervous. This man was known as the enforcer – he was the one that if anyone stepped out of line, he put them back on it.

I walked over to the table that Joe was now sitting at and I sat down.

"What is it, Joe?" I asked.

"Listen son, can I ask you, where do your loyalties lie?"

"What do you mean, Joe?"

"Your loyalties. I want to know, do you know we are at war with the I.R.A.? I want to know how you feel about that."

"Never really thought about it Joe, but now that you ask I suppose I hate them like everyone else on the Shankill. Why do you ask, Joe?"

"I want you to mind something for me. Put it somewhere safe and don't tell anyone that I have asked you to do this."

"Can I ask what it is, Joe?"

"You don't need to know just yet, son. All you need to know is that it's my bag and when I ask you, and only when I ask you, that you bring it back to me."

I didn't know what to say or what to do. I just sat

there staring at Joe.

"I will pay you for minding it, Jonny. A fiver a week after the meeting we have."

"Yeah, ok Joe. Where is it?"

"In the boot of my car, son. I will give it to you when you lock up."

I turned all the lights off and pulled the shutter down. Joe was already in his car when I locked the door. I turned and got into his car.

"Broom Street, Jonny. That's where you live, isn't it?"

"Yes Joe, it is. If you just drop me off at the bottom of the street, I don't want my ma or da seeing you give me a bag out of your boot."

"Good thinking, son. The less people know the better."

We pulled up at the bottom of my street and we both got out of the car. Joe walked to the back and opened the boot; he pulled out a grip bag and handed it to me.

"Here Jonny, put it somewhere safe and make sure nobody sees you as there are a couple of things in that bag that's important to me."

"I will, Joe. You can trust me."

"I know I can, Jonny."

Joe reached into his back pocket and pulled out his wallet; he handed me a fiver and said, "That's the first week paid, Jonny."

Joe got into his car and left me standing at the

bottom of my street. I stood there with this bag, wondering what to do with it. It was quite heavy so God knows what was in it. Knowing Joe, it was probably guns, but when I had a good look at the bag it was stitched shut so I couldn't open it.

I walked up home and in through the front door. My mum and dad were already in bed, which was a huge relief 'cause there was no way I could tell them about the deal I had with Joe.

I put the bag under my bed and lay there all night, wondering where to hide it.

The next day I just stayed in and waited for my mum and dad to go out. As soon as they had closed the front door, up the stairs I ran to get the bag.

I brought it back downstairs and put it on the kitchen table. I felt round it, trying to figure out what was in it, but it was too well packed. There was no chance of knowing what was in it unless I opened it, and the fear of what Joe would do was enough for me not to open it.

I put the bag over my shoulder and walked to my granny's house to hide it.

When I got to her house I walked on in.

"Nanny, where are you?" I shouted.

"Is that you, Jonny?" I heard her shout from up the stairs.

"Yes Nanny, it is. I need to go to your toilet."

"Oh right son, that's ok."

I walked out to the back yard and opened the toilet door. I reached round and turned the light on. I set the bag on the floor and stood up on the toilet; the bloody spiders were everywhere as usual but I had to get this bag hidden before my nanny came out. I pushed on the board that was the ceiling and moved it over slightly. I felt for the old tin to see if it was still there. Yep, still there, so I knew nobody had been here. I got back down and lifted the bag and reached it up into the gap. It fitted perfectly. I moved the board back over again and the bag was out of sight.

Just at that, my nanny came out.

"You ok, Jonny? Did you get sorted?"

"Yes Nanny, I did. I just made it. There was no way I could have made it to my house."

My nanny laughed.

"Do you want a wee cup of tea, son, and a sandwich?"

The thought of my nanny's jelly ham sandwiches was too much.

"No Nanny, I have to be somewhere. I can't stay but thanks anyway."

"No worries, son. You take care, sure I will see you Sunday as usual."

"Yeah Nanny, see you then."

And out the front door I went.

As I walked back up home it was a huge relief to get that bag out of the house and somewhere safe. There was no way my nanny would find it, her toilet hadn't been cleaned in years.

CHAPTER 18

Orange Lil And The Store Room

I really enjoyed working in Heather Street and working for Billy; there were some really good nights in the club. The nights that there was a charity do on were the best.

It was a Saturday night and Billy and me opened up for 5pm. We had to let the band in to set up but it gave us plenty of time to get the bar stocked and to sit down and listen to the band warm up. We always had a couple of pints and a chat but it wasn't long until the first people arrived to get the best seats, and that was my cue to get behind the bar.

Of course it was Orange Lil and her wee Victor, as she always called him, and up to the bar she came.

"Just the usual, Lilly?" I asked.

"Yes sexy, vodka Diet Coke for me and a pint for your man here."

As she looked over her shoulder at Victor, who was standing just behind her, nursing fresh bruises on his face, I really felt sorry for him. Lilly was awful to him, especially the weekends when she got drunk – she beat the head off him.

"You're looking very nice Jonny, in your wee tight jeans. You have a sexy wee bum."

I poured Lilly her drink.

"Aye, Lilly, you say all the right things. If I was ten years older you might have a chance but you're looking well yourself. Victor, you're a lucky man," I said, looking over at Victor. He just smiled and said nothing.

Lilly was dressed in the skimpiest mini skirt you have ever seen. I swear her arse cheeks were hanging out of the bottom of her skirt and her top, she was gonna burst out of it. I've never seen bigger boobs in my life and she wasn't wearing a bra either. It was practically see through. No matter where she was in the bar, it was like a moth to a flame; you couldn't help look at her boobs and her nipples, they would cut the eyes of you. I'm telling you, you could hang your coat on them.

As the night went on the crowd got drunker and louder. The band was super; the music they played had everyone up dancing and in between a few of the songs they tortured people with pure banter. Lilly got a real mauling about her boobs and skirt but it didn't seem to annoy her. I think it made her worse; in fact, when she was up dancing I swear one of her boobs fell out and she didn't even miss a dance step, she just threw it back in again and kept dancing. Me and Billy never laughed as much – it was pure crack.

It was during the break when the ballot was being drawn that I went into the back store to change a barrel.

The store was dimly lit as one of the lightbulbs had blown, and in middle of changing the barrel I heard the door close behind me.

"Alright Billy, who's behind the bar?" I said as I turned round to face him.

But it wasn't Billy; to my surprise it was a drunken Orange Lil.

"Lilly, what you doing back here?" I said as Lilly staggered towards me.

"Hopefully you if you play your cards right, sexy," she replied.

"Lilly, you're drunk. You shouldn't be in here. If Billy finds out I will get sacked."

"Never you mind about Billy, he's busy behind the bar. Now come over here and put your lips on me."

Holy fuck, she was taking her top off. Oh my god, she had her tits out and she was holding them as she was now standing in front of me. She grabbed my hands and put them on her tits.

"I bet you haven't felt a pair like these, Jonny?" she asked.

"No Lilly, I haven't."

She then started kissing me and she then put her hand down onto my dick. She was rubbing like I don't know what the fuck. I thought she was going to rub it off.

"Lilly, you better stop. What about Victor? You're married," I said as I tried to get her off me.

"Never mind about Victor, we haven't had sex in years. He's not interested and I have to get a bit. I'm horny as hell and you're gonna fuck me, Jonny."

As she opened up my jeans she got on her knees and yep, started sucking me off. Oh my god, what a feeling. I'd never had sex with a girl before, never mind get a blow job. Fuck, fuck, fuck. I grabbed the back of her head and pulled her closer. She stopped and stood up; my heart was thumping out of my chest.

"My turn now, Jonny," she said as she pulled her skirt up, and yep, she wasn't wearing any knickers. She lay down on the store room floor.

"Right Jonny, bring the hard on over here."

Victor was the furthest thing from my mind; my dick was pulsating, I had to have sex with her. I walked over and lay on top of her; she reached down and put my dick inside her.

"Ah, Jonny. Harder, harder," she said as she was moaning.

I was going like a rabbit on speed. *Holy fuck,* I thought, *if I go any harder or faster she's gonna burst into flames.*

It lasted what felt like ten minutes but in reality it was about two, but what a two minutes. I had never experienced anything like it. Yes, Lilly was near forty and I was only nineteen, and yes, she was about twenty stone and I was about ten stone, but between us it was thirty stone of pure bliss.

I got up off Lilly and she got up, pulled her skirt

down, and put her top back on. She said to me, "Not bad, Jonny. We should make this our wee Saturday night thing. Now mum's the word."

After she kissed her finger and touched my lips, she turned and walked out the store room door. I stood there in shock at what had just happened; I zipped my jeans back up. Just in time too as Billy came walking in.

"Jonny, I need you back out in the bar again. We are getting busy again and by the way, Lilly was looking for you."

As Billy turned and walked away I gave a sigh of relief.

"Right Billy, I'm coming now," I said, as I smiled to myself.

I walked back out and behind the bar and guess what, there was Orange Lil sitting in her usual seat at the bar with Victor just behind her, talking to some bloke. My face took a pure redner when she said to me, "Just the usual, Jonny," as she winked at me.

"Ok Lilly, get it for you now."

Billy came over.

"I will get that, Jonny." As he leaned in to whisper in my ear he said, "Go into the toilet, Jonny, you have Lilly's makeup all over you, before Victor sees you."

Again, my face went red. I turned and just walked straight into the toilet. As the door closed behind me I stood at the only mirror and sink in there. I looked at my reflection in the rusty mirror and Billy wasn't joking – I was plastered. Fuck, I thought as I turned the tap on. It was everywhere – all over my bake, on my shirt. I threw some water on my face and started rubbing it, but what sort of fucking makeup was this? It wouldn't come off. The harder and faster I rubbed, it just made it worse; my whole face was covered now. I looked like Coco the Clown.

Just at that, the door opened behind me and this drunk guy staggered in and stood at the urinal beside me. As he started pissing he turned to me.

"Alright son, trying to fix your makeup," he laughed.

"It's not mine," I said, in a real panic now.

"Big Lilly get the hold of you then," he said, again laughing.

I stopped trying to get it off and looked at him.

"Aye mate, what am I gonna do? I can't get this shit off."

"Try a bit of soap, it should come off with that."

I lifted the bar of soap and lathered it up under the water, and started washing my face. Thank fuck, it was coming off; three good washes and I was back to normal. Well, there was the case of my shirt. I took it off and turned it inside-out; it was hard to button it back up again but I managed it. It's just as well it was a plain white one, I wouldn't have gotten away with a patterned one.

Back out to the bar I went, and as I stood serving the next customer, Billy came over and again leaned in. "The old reverse shirt trick," he said as he laughed and walked off.

I looked over at him and just laughed.

After the last person had left and we got the bar cleaned up, Billy said to me.

"Well what happened between you and Orange Lil? And don't spare the details."

My face went red. "Nothing, Billy. Nothing," I stuttered.

"Aye, right. Do you think I came up the lagan in a bubble, Jonny? You better be careful with that one, she's not worth the agro, son."

I just blurted it all out. "Billy she followed me into the store and I had sex with her. What am I going to do? What if Victor finds out?"

"Calm down, Jonny. It's not Victor you need to worry about, he's just glad she stays away from him. It's Lilly you need to worry about, she's a sex maniac. Once she gets her claws into you she will want more, son. If you want my advice, avoid her like the plague and when you go into the store room lock the door behind you and you should be ok."

"I will, Billy. She's not right in the head."

"You got that right, son. Just stay away."

Billy locked up and drove me home.

CHAPTER 19

A Black Tie Day

As Billy drove the car up the street I could see blue flashing lights, and the closer we got to my street I could see a police car parked across the bottom of my street. Billy pulled the car over and we both got out. The police had our street cordoned off with tape. I walked over to the policeman.

"What's wrong, mister?" I asked as I looked up my street. I could see a fire engine parked halfway up and firemen out with the hoses. My heart thumped. They were pumping water into a house that had smoke billowing out of it. I heard one of the firemen shout, "More water! We need another hose! Get another hose quick before this fire spreads to next door!"

I tried to go under the tape but the policeman grabbed me.

"You can't go up there, son. You have to stay behind the tape."

As I looked round I could see the neighbours all out. I looked and looked but I couldn't see my mum or dad. I started panicking. I looked at Billy.

"Billy! Billy, that's my house. Where's my ma? Where's my da?"

Billy just looked at me; he didn't know what to say.

I shouted, "Ma! Ma, where are you?"

I took to my heels and under the tape I went. I ran up the street. It was my house; the flames were coming out of the top windows. The firemen were in a real panic – one man was on a hose pumping water in through the front window and two other firemen were putting masks on. I heard another fireman say, "You got to go in, there is people in there."

"Ma! Da! Where are yous?" I shouted.

And just at that, the policeman grabbed me.

"I told you, you can't be up here."

I turned and looked at him. I saw Billy run up the street and when he got to the policeman he said, "Get your hands off him, his mum and dad is in there."

Billy grabbed the policeman's arm and pulled him away.

As I stood there in floods of tears, and with one of the hoses from the fire engine spraying water all over me, I was soaked to the skin. I was devastated; I couldn't control myself. I fell to my knees, crying and screaming for my mum. Billy came over and put his arm round me. He was as soaked as I was but he crouched down and I could hear him talk but didn't know what he was saying. I just couldn't stop crying. I sat and watched as the firemen put the flames out and still, I was shouting. Billy did his best to calm me down but he was in tears as well so we both just sat there in the soaked street, not knowing what to do or say.

After a while the policeman came over.

"Billy, you and the lad will have to move back a bit. I know it's hard but you will have to let the firemen do their job."

Billy looked at me.

"Jonny, get up, son. We have to move back a bit."

By now the street was full of people and I had stopped crying. Billy and me and some of the neighbours stood opposite my house, and the realisation of what had just happened was upon us all. The house was gutted; the smoke was still coming out of the top windows but the flames were out. Just at that, two firemen came out of the house. I heard one of them say, "We need a bag, we found a body."

I bolted over to them. Billy tried his best to hold me but nothing was keeping me out of the house. I ran past the two firemen and into our living room.

I heard the firemen shout, "Don't go in there, son! It's too dangerous."

I ignored their shouts as I stood in my house. Everything went silent; the room was black, the floor filled with water, but as I looked round I saw my da lying on the sofa. He was just lying there. It looked like he was just sleeping. He was stinking with black soot but he wasn't burnt. I shouted out as I walked towards him, "Da! DA! Wake up!"

I shook him.

"Da! Da! Open your eyes."

Just at that, I felt a hand on my shoulder.

"Son, your da's gone. He is dead, son."

I looked round and standing there was a fireman. He said to me, "Come on son. This house isn't safe. We got to get you out of here."

I just threw myself onto my da, trying to get him to wake up. I was screaming and crying.

"Da! Get up! Get up, Da!"

I was sobbing as the fireman put his arm around me and we walked out of my house. As I got out onto the street I saw Billy standing there. I couldn't really see him, the tears were blinding me. I just couldn't stop crying, but I heard him say. "Jonny! Jonny, your mum's here."

I looked up and my mum was standing with Billy. I ran over and threw my arms round her.

"Ma! Ma, you're ok. I thought you were in the house."

I hugged her really tightly. We stood there, both crying, and then she said to me, "Jonny I was at your nanny's. I should have come home but your da was in there."

"I know, Ma. He's dead. He's lying on the sofa."

She hugged me again.

A car came up the street and just at that, two firemen came walking out of our house carrying a body bag with my da in it. They put it in the back of a big black hearse and the man came over to speak with my mum.

"Mrs Andrews, I am Tony Black. I am bringing

your husband's body to the Mater Hospital where the coroner will have to do tests on him."

"Why? He is dead. Why do they have to do tests?" my mum asked.

"To find out the cause of death, Mrs Andrews. It's just a formality."

When the car drove off we just stood there looking at its brake lights as it turned the corner at the bottom of our street.

That night we stayed in my nanny's house. The fire had started when my da came home from the bar and he decided to make himself chips. He had put the chip pan on and had fell asleep on the sofa when it took hold. The coroner's report said that it was the smoke that killed him, which was a wee bit easier to take as my mum and I knew then he had died in his sleep.

We moved into my nanny's as we had nowhere else to go, and it was Friday when my da was to be buried.

I woke up early and went downstairs. My nanny and mum were already up making breakfast.

"Morning son, how are you?" my mum asked as she poured three cups of tea.

"Ok Mum, are you ok?" I asked.

"Yes son. It's going to be a hard day today but we will get through it."

My nanny turned and said, "Do you want some toast, Jonny?"

"Yes Nanny, I would love some."

The three of us sat round my nanny's wee table

and ate our breakfast. We hardly spoke a word as today we were going to say goodbye to my dad.

After breakfast I went into my nanny's front room where my dad was in lying in a coffin. He was dressed in a dark grey suit with a shirt and tie; I stood there in front of him. He really did look well. I thought to myself, *Da, why did you not wake up? You must have smelt the smoke. How are we going to get through life without you? Where are we going to live? How is my mum going to cope?* Just at that my mum came in. I turned to face her; the tears were running down my face.

"It's ok, Jonny. It's ok, son, to cry."

She put her arms round me and gave me a hug.

"What are we going to do, Ma? Where are we going to live?"

"We will live with your nanny for a while until we get a new place. Don't worry, son. We will be fine."

"But Ma, what about you? Are you going to be ok?"

"To be honest, son, and don't tell anyone this, I was leaving your da anyway. I was fed up with his drinking and being on the end of his tempers. I went round to your nanny's that night of the fire to bring some of our stuff. I had put up with it for far too long. If your da hadn't died in that fire you probably would have been burying me, as I couldn't take it anymore. Now promise me this, Jonny, you won't breathe a word of this to anyone. As much as your da was bad to me he also was good, but I am not sorry he's gone. I'm just sorry it turned out like this and you losing your dad, but I hope you understand. I won't shed another tear over him. We will give him a good send-off and just move on with our lives."

"I know, Ma. I heard him hit you most weekends and sometimes I wished him dead, so I think it's my fault he died in that fire."

"Stop right there, Jonny. It's not your fault. Never think like that. Your da never thought of anyone but himself – nobody forced him to drink. You never deserved being on the end of him hitting you and I certainly didn't deserve to be cleaning up his crap when he came home drunk and dealing with paying his debts off to the U.V.F. I won't miss any of that and you know what, wait and see how many people today say how much he was a great man and how many people say how much they are going to miss him. I'm telling you this, I can't wait to get to bed tonight."

Just at that, a knock came to the door. It was a couple of the neighbours from our street.

"Come on in," I heard my nanny say.

The two women came walking into my nanny's front room where me and my ma were.

"Alright Annie, how are you holding up?" one of the women asked.

"We are doing ok, Jean."

"We had a collection in the area for you and Jonny and we wanted to give it to you before the funeral to help with the bills."

As Jean handed my mum a bag of money my mum said, "That's too kind, Jean. Thank you so much, it means a lot to me and Jonny that yous are all thinking of us on this day."

"Listen Annie, if there is anything you need, just ask. We are all here to support you and Jonny and whatever it takes, we will all help."

"Again Jean, thanks, but we will be fine. Are you going back to Heather Street after the funeral? Billy is putting a spread on for everyone."

"Yes Annie, we are all going back. I wouldn't miss it."

"That's good. Sure I will catch up with you there for a natter."

And my mum ushered Jean and Betty out the front door.

She looked at me. "Jonny, we are going to be fine, now go up and get washed and get yourself dressed. I left a suit out for you to put on. The funeral directors will be here in an hour so you may get your skates on."

"Ok Ma." I gave her a hug and I went upstairs to get ready.

It wasn't long before a knock came to the door and the funeral directors had arrived. Then a pastor from our local church came and spoke with my mum about how things were to run today. I came downstairs dressed in the most beautiful suit I had ever seen, a bright white shirt, and a black tie. My mum was standing at the front door, welcoming people who had turned up for my da's funeral. She turned when she heard me walk down the stairs; she started crying as I got to the bottom of my nanny's stairs. She threw her arms round me and whispered in my ear, "Jonny, you're a man. Look at you, you're not my wee boy anymore."

"Ma, I am always going to be your wee boy, that will never change. Now come on, let's get my da up the road."

When I looked outside the street was black with people. There were too many people to recognise anyone but I couldn't get over the crowd that was there. I came back inside and stood with my mum and nanny as the pastor said a few words about my da and we prayed. I held my mum's hand really tightly and fought back the tears. When it was time to bring my da outside the funeral directors asked everyone to go out and they carefully lifted the coffin out of my nanny's front room.

I took the first lift, along with three other men, and we walked out onto Tennett Street. There were two other lifts which took us out onto the Shankill and up to the Mountain View club where my da always went and drank. When we got up to the bar we stopped and all the men that were in the bar came out and stood as my da lay in his coffin. One by one the men came over; they stood round him and one of them put an Ulster flag on it. Another man came out of the bar with a balaclava on, dressed in combat gear. He marched over, carrying a rifle. The men parted in all directions of my da's coffin and created a gap; the man proceeded over to my da and pointed his rifle in the air. Another man spoke.

"Here lies a soldier of the U.V.F., Jimmy Andrews, and he will be remembered."

Just at that, the man with the rifle fired three times over his coffin. It made me jump and I just looked at my mum, and she looked at me. We never spoke but the two of us had no idea that my da was in the U.V.F.

All those times he said he was away to the bar, we never knew what he was doing or who he was with. We just thought he was with his drinking buddies.

The men all went back into the Mountain View and my da's coffin was put in the back of the hearse.

My mum, nanny, and me got into another big black car and followed the hearse to the graveyard where my da was laid to rest.

When we got back to Heather Street Social Club Billy had laid on a spread of food and drinks for everyone. I couldn't have thanked him enough. He did my ma proud; everyone there stuffed their faces and had a couple of drinks.

It was a really long day so I was glad it was over, and I was lying in my bed in my nanny's house.

CHAPTER 20

The Itch

A few days passed. We had settled into my nanny's house and with the money the community had raised my mum was able to get us some clothes and make a start on getting furniture for our new house, which was just five doors away from my nanny's. We were due to move there in about two weeks when the housing executive had it ready for us. An old man had lived in it but he was moved into a nursing home as he wasn't well and wouldn't be back, so me and my mum got it and it couldn't have come quicker, as I think my nanny's house wasn't big enough for all of us. As it was a two-bedroom house my mum was sleeping on the sofa in her front room and it wasn't doing her bad back any good.

I started back at work as we needed the money. Billy was great; he kept my job for me even though he could have done with the help when I was off, but to be honest I couldn't stay off a minute longer as my nanny was starting to do my head in. I couldn't even go for a piss, she was following me asking if I was ok.

It was Saturday night and I got to the bar for about four to help Billy stock up. We were due a delivery from the brewery and it all had to be hand balled in, so it was a bit of work but it kept me busy and kept my mind off my nanny and ma.

"Jonny, good to have you back, son. I have really missed you. My bloody back is broke with all the extra work. How's the form anyway, son?" Billy asked.

"Filled in and sent away, Billy," I replied with one of Nigel's aul sayings.

Billy laughed. "Not bad, Jonny. Not bad, son."

We got the delivery brought in and started filling the fridges.

"Have you had any dinner yet, Jonny?"

"No Billy, I haven't."

Billy handed me a tenner. "Away down to the chippers and get two suppers, son. Put gravy on mine."

I went down the street and got us our dinner. When I came back up to the bar Billy had everything done and we sat down with the nicest pint I had ever tasted, and the fish and chips went down well as well.

It wasn't long before the guy who was doing the entertainment arrived, and he set up in the usual place. He sat on a stool and tuned up his guitar and belted out a couple of Kenny Rogers tunes. I had a wee smile to myself as it brought back memories of my da being half drunk walking up our street singing his heart out. It was nice having those thoughts.

"Right Jonny, open the doors, son. It's 7 o'clock, let's get this show on the road."

It wasn't too long before the usual punters came in and by 8 o'clock the bar was in full swing, and guess who was in her usual seat at the bar. Yep, Orange Lil with her wee Victor.

"Alright Jonny, love. How you been keeping?"

"Ok Lilly, glad to be back to work."

"So am I, sexy. I have missed that wee sexy bum in them tight jeans."

"Aye Lilly, what would you like to drink?"

"Just the usual, Jonny, but make mine a double."

I poured the drinks and tried hard not to encourage her, but it doesn't take much for Lilly; she tortured the life out of me. I swear I really didn't know how Victor sticks her. She was absolutely filthy; the things she said were obscene and she had her usual clothes on – well, lack of clothes. I thought to myself, *She really should invest in a bra that actually fits her.* The one she had on was so tight I swear her boobs were pushed so far up they were about to fall out of her top.

I did my best to avoid her and when I had to go and change a barrel I took Billy's advice and kept the door locked behind me in case Lilly got up to her old tricks. Speaking of which, since that night in the store room my dick had been aching. I couldn't stop scratching. I swear at times I could scratch it right off.

Later on that night, just before the guy sang the last song, I had to nip to the toilet. I said to Billy I had to go and asked if he was ok behind the bar. He nodded and said, "Don't be too long." Last orders were in ten minutes.

I went into the cubicle and had just pulled the door over when a bright red high-heeled shoe stopped me from closing it. I opened the door and there stood Orange Lil with her skirt pulled up round her neck.

"Round two, Jonny lad."

"Fuck's sake Lilly, you can't be in here and fir fuck's sake pull your skirt down before somebody comes in."

"Nobody will come in, I have locked the door. Now come over here and give me what I need."

"Fir fuck's sake, Lilly. I just buried my da last week, give me a break. I'm not doing this."

As I pushed past her and walked out the door, Victor was standing waiting for her to come out.

"What's wrong, Jonny? Are you in a bit of a rush?"

"Fuck's sake Victor that wife of yours needs a leash put on her. How the fuck do you put up with her?"

And that was the last thing I remembered until I came round. Billy was standing over me and a few other people as well.

"Jonny, are you ok, son?"

"Billy, what happened?"

"Victor punched you, son. What did you say to him?"

As I got to my feet I was still dazed.

"Sit down, son," I heard someone from behind me

say. As I looked round, I saw it was Joe the enforcer. I sat down and Billy handed me a tea towel full of ice. I held it to my eye which was now swollen and bloody sore.

"What happened, Jonny?" Billy asked again.

"Orange Lil followed me into the toilet, Billy, and tried it on again. I told her no chance and came back out here but Victor was standing holding the door shut. I told him that Lilly needs a leash put on and he didn't take it too well. I didn't even see it coming."

"You made a mistake there, son. Victor used to be a boxer and he can fight like fuck," Billy replied. "You're lucky he only hit you once. It was Lilly that pulled him away and the two of them went home."

"Fuck, Billy you could of warned me."

"I did, son. I told you to stay away from her, she is bad news. You're not the first, son, and as sure as hell you won't be the last."

I got to my feet and got myself together. We cleaned up and got the hangers on out the door.

"Billy, can I ask you something?"

"Aye Jonny, what's wrong?"

"I have this itch and it's driving me crazy."

"Where's your itch, son?"

"My dick and balls, Billy. I could tear strips off them."

"Oh dear. Son, I think a wee trip to the doctors is required. Ask your ma to make you an appointment."

"No way, Billy. I couldn't, I would be scundered.

She would probably ask to see them and what would I do then?"

Billy laughed. "Fir God's sake, Jonny. What are you like? If you go down on Monday morning to the doctors and ask to see the nurse in the treatment room, she will sort you out."

As we walked to Billy's car the thought of a nurse looking at my private bits was really worrying me. What if she was good looking and I took a hard on? Holy fuck, what would I do?

Billy dropped me off home and I went straight to bed before my nanny or ma saw my swollen eye.

The next morning was two thousand questions, and the best excuse I came up with was that a fight broke out in the bar and I caught a stray punch trying to break it up. There was no way I could tell the truth that I had a run-in with Victor, and all the antics of Lilly and her torturing me for sex.

I just lurched about the house that day. I couldn't stop scratching, it was driving me nuts. Even my ma said to me, "For frig's sake, Jonny. You're making me itchy, will you stop scratching?" My face went a pure redner.

Monday morning and down to the doctors. It was usual Nor'n Ireland weather, pissing out of the heavens, so by the time I got down to the doctors I was soaked to the skin. My eye was now turning black and still swollen, so I looked well. When I walked through the front doors I felt like a total edgit. I looked like a drowned rat that had done a few rounds with Nigel Benn, the Dark Destroyer, who I loved watching when Billy put a fight night on in the club.

I went up to the girl in reception and asked if I could see the nurse in the treatment room. She gave me a ticket and told me to take a seat and listen for my number to be called. I was sweating it in case she wanted to know what it was for. In my head I was going to use my eye as the excuse but she didn't ask so I was chuffed.

I sat there in the crowded room waiting my turn, and the itching was terrible. I couldn't sit still. The wee woman next to me said, "What's wrong, son? Ants in your pants?"

"No missus, just soaked through and I'm freezing."

"Aye, love the weather – shocking. What number are you?"

As I looked at my ticket, it read '14'. *Fuck me, I'm gonna be here all day.*

"Fourteen missus, looks like I'm gonna be a while."

"Here love, swap tickets. I'm next I think." And she handed me her ticket. It read '4'.

"Are you sure, missus?" I said, as the itching was getting unbearable.

"Yes love, I'm in no rush and you're soaked. You need to get away home and get out of them wet clothes."

Just at that, a girl came out of the treatment room; she called, "Number four."

I thanked the woman and gave her my ticket. As I looked at the girl who called the number I nearly passed out. She was gorgeous. She looked about my age, blonde hair, class figure. It was my worst nightmare. The thought of me getting my bits out for her to exam was frightening the life out of me. I just stood there. She said again, "Number four."

I replied, "Yes," and handed her the ticket.

"Come on in, I won't bite." And she smiled.

Her teeth were bright white, she had blue eyes, her makeup was perfect. To be honest, I fancied the life out of her – she was stunning. She was wearing a tight pair of jeans and a white jacket with her name tag on it. I was now going bright red but I managed to read it and her name was Karen.

"Hi Karen, I'm here to see the nurse," I said, praying it wasn't her.

She replied, "What's your name and who is your doctor?"

"Jonny Andrews, and my doctor is Doctor Beck."

As she turned and walked towards a desk, I caught a glimpse of her bum – she was a full ten. She sat at the desk and said to me, "Take a seat here, Jonny. I need a few more details of you before the nurse will see you."

I sat at the desk beside Karen and the smell of her perfume was lovely. I don't know why but I asked her, "Your perfume is lovely. What is it?"

She turned and smiled.

"It's Paris, I got it down the town."

"It's really nice."

She blushed a bit but not even close to my face. I looked like I had sat too close to the fire.

Karen turned back to the computer.

"Found you. Are you still living in Broom Street?"

"No I'm not. I've moved round to Orkney Street, number twenty-seven."

"Oh right, I will update that as well for you."

And there it was, the dreaded question.

"And what seems to be the problem?" she asked, as she was typing on the computer.

My head dropped and I mumbled, "I have an itch."

"Sorry, what? I didn't catch that, Jonny."

Shit. My face felt on fire. I lifted my head.

"I have an itch," I repeated.

"And where is this itch?" She stopped typing and turned to face me. "Don't be embarrassed, Jonny. I have heard everything in here. I need to know so we can get you treated."

"Um, it's down below," I stuttered, and pointed to my balls.

"Oh right, and have you any idea how it started? For example, have you had sex with anyone?"

I sat there, this gorgeous girl in front of me, and I'm about to tell her about Orange Lil.

"No, I really don't know. I just know it's driving me crazy. I can hardly get a night's sleep with scratching."

"Oh right, we will get the nurse to take a look."

And just at that, another door opened and stood there was this aul doll with glasses on, dressed in the most flowery dress I had ever seen. To be honest it looked like a pair of curtains that hung in my nanny's front room.

"Jonny Andrews, can you come in here?"

I stood up. "Here goes nothing," I said to Karen.

She smiled. "You will be fine."

I walked into the treatment room; the nurse asked me to remove my trousers and pants and she got me to lie down on a bed. When she started examining me, she said, "Oh dear, that looks nasty. How long has it been like this?" As she lifted my penis up, I flinched. "Oh, sorry Jonny. Are my hands cold?"

"Just a bit." But in my mind was, *Don't take a hard on, don't take a hard on.*

"It's been like this for about a week now, it's really itchy."

"I'm sure it is, son. You caught a sexually transmitted disease."

"What! Is it serious?" I asked, really panicking.

"Serious enough. If we don't treat it I'm going to have to take a couple of samples to be tested."

"Am I going to die?" I asked.

"No Jonny, you're going to have to lay off sex for a while until we get this cleared up." She went into a drawer and lifted out a packet. "I'm going to have to take a scraping of the inside of your penis – it might hurt a bit."

As I lay there on the bed she shoved something up my penis, which wasn't too bad but when she pulled it out I thought my dick was going to fall off.

"Fuck," I said. "That's really sore."

"I know, son, but it has to be done."

"That's you, you can get dressed."

She sat at her desk writing out a prescription.

"You need to go and get these, it's an antibiotic and a cream as well to help clear that itch up."

She also reached into the bottom drawer and pulled out a box.

"And here, next time you're going to have sex, make sure you use one of these."

My face was beaming as she handed me the prescription and a box of condoms.

"Thanks, I will do, and thanks for the advice."

As I walked back out Karen was standing.

"Well, did you get sorted?"

"Yes, I did thanks."

I stood there with my box of condoms, this gorgeous girl in front of me; it couldn't have been more awkward.

"Do you want a bag for them?" she asked as she pointed to the box.

"Yes please, you would be a life saver. I don't fancy walking through reception with these."

Karen laughed as she handed me a bag.

"I work up in Heather Street club. If you ever want to call in I would buy you a drink."

"I might do that some night, but it might be a bit awkward as I live over in East Belfast."

"Why would it be awkward, Karen?"

"My da wouldn't let me drink on the Shankill."

"What about we go into town some night? Nothing serious, maybe the cinema?"

"Aye, we could do that," she replied.

I gave her the biggest smile I had smiled for a long time.

"You're on. What about Thursday night? I could meet you in town where the buses drop you off?"

"Yeah, that's fine, 6pm ok?"

"Perfect. I will see you then."

As I walked out of the doctors I had the biggest cheezer you would have ever seen. I just got a date with a stunner. I walked straight into the chemist next door and got my prescription, and as I dandered up home my knob was throbbing but I didn't care, it was well worth the pain to get a date with Karen.

That night I started work in the bar. As I walked in, Billy was busy as usual getting set up. It was darts night so nothing too serious. As I hung my coat up in the store, Billy called me.

"Jonny, can you come here a minute?"

I turned to see he was standing with Victor. Fuck, I thought Victor was down to hit me again. The blood drained from me.

"What is it, Billy?"

"Victor here has something to say to you, son."

"Jonny, it's about the other night. I'm really sorry, son. It wasn't your fault, I just couldn't take Lilly's antics anymore, son, and you got the brunt of it."

"It's ok, Victor. I shouldn't of said what I did. I was out of order."

"No, son. You were bang on and it took you to get me to wake up. I had words with Lilly and I assure you she won't be bothering you again."

"Thanks Victor, are we ok?"

"Yes son, we are fine. I'm just sorry I hit you."

"It's ok, Victor. I will get over it."

And just at that, we shook hands and Billy had set us up a pint each.

This day couldn't get any better. That pint was the sweetest drink I had ever tasted; it went down a charm. I set the rest of the bar up just in time for when the darts teams arrived, and started pouring the drinks. My itch was still as bad and Billy noticed me scratching.

"Did you go to the doctors this morning, Jonny, and get something for that itch?"

"Aye Billy, I did, but it's gonna take a while to get it cleared up."

"What did they say it was, Jonny?" and Billy gave a laugh.

"Billy, I caught something off Lilly. She said it was a sexually transmitted disease."

Billy leant in. "Jonny, take a look around the bar. Take a good look."

"What do you mean, Billy?"

"Just take a look."

As I stood there behind the bar I looked at all the men who were either playing darts or just watching, and it hit me.

"Fuck me, Billy. Half the bar is scratching."

"Shush. Keep it down, Jonny."

"Yep, our Lilly has been a busy girl. I told you, you weren't her first but it looks like what Victor was saying, you certainly are her last." And he stood there laughing.

CHAPTER 21

The Date

Thursday couldn't have come any quicker; I couldn't wait to see Karen again. I had asked Billy for the night off so after my dinner I went and put my favourite jeans and shirt on, lifted my denim jacket, and just as I was about to go out the front door, my ma spotted me.

"Hey boy, where are you going all dressed up on a Thursday night?"

"I'm meeting a girl, Ma, in town. We are going to the cinema."

"Oh, hot date. You're smelling well, she must be a looker."

"Aye Ma, she is. I met her the other day down the road and we just clicked so I asked her to go to the cinema with me."

"Watch yourself in town and have a nice night,

son. Have you got enough money?"

"Yes Ma, I have," and out the door I went.

I walked onto the road and jumped a black hack. It dropped me off in lower North Street so a quick dander through town and onto the Lisburn road where I had arranged to meet Karen. I was about ten minutes early so as I sat on the wall next to the cinema, I was fixated on my watch. As I looked down, I heard, "Hi Jonny, have you been waiting long?"

I looked up my heart missed a beat – it was Karen. "Hi Karen. No, not at all. How are you?"

As I looked her up and down, she was stunning. Her long blonde hair rested on her shoulders; she was wearing a blue jacket, a nice white top, and tight blue jeans. She was gorgeous, standing there, I swear my eyes near popped out.

"Yeah I'm fine, just glad to get a night out. What about you? I see your eye has cleared up."

"Aye, it's fine. I'm glad of a night off and all the better for seeing you."

"Just the charmer, aren't you?" she laughed. "What would you like to see?" she asked.

As we stood there looking up at the billboard we decided to watch The Wedding Singer. A bit of a chick flick but sure I would have watched a blank screen if it meant I was with her.

As we stood in the queue I heard a familiar voice.

"Jonny Andrews, is that you?"

I turned, and who was there?

"Gerrerd, what about you mate? Long time no see."

Gerrerd was standing there with a girl, she was not bad looking either. He had shaved his ginger hair off and was a monster of a lad now. He must have been six foot tall.

"Aye Jonny, how have you been?"

"Alright mate, this is Karen," I said, and I turned to Karen. "Karen, this is my mate Gerrerd. We used to play football together."

"Hiya Gerrerd," Karen replied.

"Jonny, this is Sonya my girlfriend." Just at that, Sonya give him a nudge.

"Excuse me, Gerrerd. Fiancée."

"Sorry Jonny, this is Sonya, my fiancée. We are getting married next year."

"Congratulations. You're a lucky man, Gerrerd."

Just at that, Sonya smiled and held his hand. Gerrerd winked at me. "So Jonny, what have you been doing with yourself? Are you back playing again?"

"No mate, I never kicked a ball again after the bomb."

"Shame, Jonny. I heard Linfield were in for you too. Bloody terrible you got caught up in that but least you're here to talk about it."

"Aye, I know mate. What about you? Are you still playing?"

"Aye mate, I got a contract at Cliftonville."

"That's brilliant mate. I always knew you would hit the big time."

"You're too kind, Jonny, but thanks. What yous

going to watch?"

"Wedding Singer, mate. What about yous?"

"Same, mate. Bloody chick flick."

"Now Gerrerd, you think you're all hard. It was you that picked it," Sonya said.

We all stood there laughing at Gerrerd's expense. As the queue went down we all paid in and joined the queue for the sweets.

When it was mine and Karen's turn I asked her what she would like.

"Anything nice you want, Karen?"

"No, I'm fine, just get yourself."

"Can I have two Cokes, some popcorn, and a couple of bars of Dairy Milk please?"

"Jonny, honestly I'm fine," Karen said.

"It's my treat, Karen."

"Thanks Jonny, that's nice of you."

I was beaming. I felt as tall as Gerrerd was, standing there with Karen beside me. The girl behind the counter got our drinks and sweets and I paid her; we stood waiting on Gerrerd and Sonya and then went in and sat down near the back.

When the film started I held Karen's hand for a while. She squeezed it a couple of times. I wasn't sure wither she liked holding my hand or couldn't wait to get stuck into the popcorn, so I squeezed her hand back and then offered her some. She took a couple of bits and ate them.

"They are lovely, Jonny. Try some?"

I lifted a handful and threw them into my mouth. Half went in an half went round me.

"Good shot, Jonny. How could you miss a mouth that big?" Karen asked, giving a wee laugh.

I was scundered. *Well done,* I thought to myself. *Real smooth, Jonny.* I laughed and said, "Ano, Karen." As I brushed the popcorn onto the floor, Gerrerd just looked at me and laughed.

I lifted my Coke and had a drink, only the lights were down. She would have seen my bright red face. I didn't eat any more popcorn, I just had my bar of chocolate and Coke. Near the end of the movie I held Karen's hand – it was great. We exchanged a couple of glances as we watched the movie and I fancied the life out of her; she was really lovely. She had a nice way with her, not like the girls I had been with before. They were rough as anything but Karen had a bit of class. I didn't want this night to end.

But end it did. As walked out of the cinema we said goodbye to Gerrerd and Sonya and I said to Karen, "How are you getting home?"

"My dad is coming to pick me up at eleven."

I looked at my watch and it read 9.45 – brilliant.

"Would you like to go for a drink?"

"Yeah, Jonny. I would like that."

We walked across the road and into a wee bar; we sat down.

"What would you like to drink?" I asked.

"A glass of cider, please, and can you get him to put a dash of blackcurrant in it?"

"Yeah, no worries."

I walked over to the bar and got Karen hers, and myself a pint. When I returned to the table Karen had taken her jacket off. I nearly lost my eyes, and to make it worse I nearly dropped the drinks as well. Karen laughed.

"Easy there, Jonny. Watch you don't spill them."

A quick side step and catastrophe avoided. Karen was beautiful when she smiled – she had a real glow about her.

I sat down opposite her and took my jacket off.

"So how long have you lived over in the east?"

"All my life. What about you? How long have you lived on the Shankill?"

"All my days as well."

We sat there talking for ages; Karen told me she had a younger sister and her mum worked in the Strand cinema and her dad used to play for Linfield. When she told me that my ears pricked up. I started telling her about Linfield wanting to sign me and then about the Shankill bomb. She was really sympathetic about that time of my life and leant across the table and gave me a kiss.

"I'm glad you're still here, Jonny, and you weren't killed in that bomb," she said.

When her lips met mine it was like time stood still. *Oh my god,* I thought. *I'm falling for this girl.*

I glanced at my watch and it read 10.50.

"It's ten to ten, Karen. Where is your da picking you up?"

"Just outside the cinema, Jonny. Would you like to take my telephone number and give me a ring?"

"Yeah," I replied.

I swear I hadn't moved as fast in my life. I was up to the bar to get a pen and back before you could say Fanny's your aunt and Dick's your uncle.

I wrote Karen's number on my hand and we finished off our drinks and went over to meet her dad. I was praying he would be late, and guess what? My prayers were answered. It was ten past eleven before he turned up, so I was able to steal a couple more snogs before he pulled up in a red Escort. As I stood there, when Karen opened the door of the car she called me over.

"Jonny, come here a minute to meet my dad."

Shit, I was scundered but I walked over and leant down. As Karen was now sitting in the front seat, she said, "Jonny, this is my dad, Alan. Dad, this is Jonny."

"Alright sir," I said, really embarrassed.

"You ok, son? How are you getting home?" he replied.

"Probably dander."

"No you're not. Jump in, son – I will run you home."

"Are you sure? I don't mind walking."

"Yes son – jump in."

I got into the back of his car and Alan drove off. Karen put her left hand round the back of the seat and I held it.

Her dad asked me, "Where do you live, son?"

"Just off Tennett Street," I replied.

"I know it well, I've been to a few dos up the Shankill."

"Yeah, Karen was telling me you played for Linfield."

"Aye son, the good old days, a bit before your time."

As we drove up the Shankill I never let go of Karen's hand. I really fancied this girl and I got the feeling she felt the same. As we pulled into Tennett Street I said to Alan, "Anywhere here will do, Alan."

As the car drew to a halt I gave Karen's hand a wee squeeze and said, "Thank you very much, I really appreciate the lift home. Karen, I will give you a ring tomorrow night about six if that's ok?"

"Yeah that's fine, Jonny. I will speak to you then."

I closed the door and Alan pulled away. I dandered up my street, smiling from ear to ear; I really enjoyed being with Karen, she really made me feel good about myself.

When I walked in through the front door my mum was sitting waiting for me.

"Well Jonny, how did the big date go?"

"Really good, Mum. Karen is lovely. She is from East Belfast and her dad used to play for Linfield."

I was just rabbiting on and on.

"Slow down, Jonny. Your mouth is going a mile a minute. You tell me she is nice then."

"Yeah Ma, she's lovely. I have to ring her tomorrow."

And as I looked at my hand my heart fell to the floor. Her number was all smudged after holding her hand in the car.

"Shit, Ma I've lost her number. What am I gonna do?"

"Let me see, son."

I showed my mum what was left of Karen's number.

"Yep, that's a big problem for you, son. Where did you say you met her?"

"Um... Um, down the road." I could feel my face go red.

"I know you said down the road. Does she work in a shop?"

That was my get out. "Yeah Ma, she does. I will call down tomorrow and see her."

"There you go, problem solved."

And off to bed I went.

The next morning I was up with the birds. I couldn't sleep; I needed to get down the road before the doctors opened at 9 so at 7.30 I got up and got ready. My mum was still in bed so I tiptoed down the stairs and made some breakfast. I started walking down the road about 8.15 and it took me a good twenty minutes to get to the doctors. I sat on a wall opposite the entrance and just waited for Karen to arrive.

As time went by people started arriving, but no Karen. At 9.30 I was really worried where she was so I walked into the reception and asked the girl behind the counter, “Excuse me but could you tell me is Karen working today?”

The woman lifted her head from the computer. She tilted her glasses and said, “No son, she isn’t.”

“Is she working tomorrow?”

“No son, she has been transferred over to the Hollywood Road health centre. She won’t be back over here.”

My jaw hit the floor, my stomach churning. I felt I was going to be sick.

“Are you ok son? You have went a bad colour,” she asked.

“I really needed to speak with her.”

“Hold on, I think I have a contact number for her.”

My heart was thumping. I thought to myself, *Please, please have her number.*

“Yes, here it is. Hold on and I will write it down for you.”

I had a big grin on my face as the woman handed me a piece of paper with Karen’s telephone number on it.

“Thank you so much, you’re a life saver,” I said as I walked back out of the door and dandered back up home.

As I walked up past the Co-op my mum was coming out with four bags of shopping.

“Here Ma, give me them, they look heavy.”

“Good timing Jonny, you’re a wee gem. My back is broke carrying them.”

"Well, did you see Karen?" she asked.

"No Ma, but I got her number and I won't lose it this time. Ma, what have you got in these bags, bloody bricks?"

"Just some messages, son."

"Jesus Ma, these would pull the back out of a donkey."

And we both laughed, walking back up home.

Later on that day I rang Karen and we chatted for ages. She told me that she had switched jobs and was over working near where she lived, so it was easier getting to and from work –she didn't have to rely on lifts. This got me thinking I had to learn to drive and get myself a wee car.

At work that night there was a football do on so it was really busy. Lilly and Victor were in and I was shocked when I saw her. She was actually looking well – no short skirts or revealing tops. She looked quite sensible when she walked up to the bar.

"Alright Jonny, how have you been?"

"Dead on, Lilly. What about you?"

Victor was standing by her side and the next words that came out of her mouth shocked the shit clean out of me.

"Me and Victor is going to have a baby. I'm pregnant."

I was speechless; Victor stood there smiling. I couldn't say anything but, "Congratulations. That's super news."

"What would you like to drink?"

"I will just have a Diet Coke and get Victor his usual."

"No worries." I poured their drinks.

As Victor turned to walk away and Lilly took a tenner out of her purse. She leant forward.

"Don't worry, Jonny. I won't say a word to Victor. He believes it's his but you and me know better." She winked and said, "Keep the change, good looking."

I was shell shocked. What the fuck? I had to get out of there. Lilly pregnant and she says it's mine? Oh my god, what was I going to do if Victor found out? He would kill me. I had to get out. Just at that, Billy walked over.

"What's up Jonny? You look flustered."

"Fuck's sake Billy, Lilly is pregnant and she says it's mine."

"Don't believe a word comes out of her mouth, son. It could be one of a dozen fellas in here, never mind the rest of the road. Our Lilly is the Belfast bike, son, so calm down. The chances are it's definitely not yours."

"Do you think so, Billy? I'm shitting myself."

"Yes son, now forget about her and stay away. She is playing mind games with you."

I couldn't concentrate all night. It couldn't have come any quicker when the last person was thrown out and we locked up.

I had arranged to meet Karen the next afternoon in town for lunch and a walk round the shops; she was heading out with her mates that night and needed to get something to wear.

It was about 12.30 and I met her at City Hall.

"Hi Karen, how's you?"

She was wearing nice blue jeans and a black top. I swear that girl would look good in a bin bag.

"Yeah, I'm fine Jonny. What about you?"

"Aye, dead on. Where would you like to go for lunch?"

"Anywhere does me. What do you fancy?"

Fancy the life out of you, I thought. "Do you just want to go to McDonalds?"

"Yeah, that would do rightly."

And we walked down Royal Avenue and in to get burger and chips.

After we had lunch we walked round a few shops until Karen got something to wear out that night.

"Where are you going tonight?" I asked.

"Me and a few mates are heading into town. I think we are to the bot up the Lisburn road."

"Is it any good?"

"Yeah, it's ok but full of married men looking to cheat on their wives, so it does my head in but the music is good."

"Nightmare, you must get tortured."

"Yeah, I do a bit but I have no interest. Sure, I have you now."

And she held my hand as we walked back up Royal Avenue to get Karen her bus home.

I gave Karen a kiss and she got on the bus over home. I just dandered up home, nothing much else to do, and as I walked up lower North Street I heard a car horn and a familiar voice shouting, "Hey boy, where you going?"

As I turned to see who it was, there, parked in his big red lorry, was Nigel. I smiled and walked over.

"Alright Nigel, how the hell have you been?"

"Alright son, haven't see you in a while. How's your mum keeping?"

"Yeah, all good Nigel. We live not far from my nanny's now in Orkney Street. We are both doing fine. How's the run going? Still as busy?"

"Aye son, busy enough. Do you want a lift up the road?"

"No Nigel, I'm fine. I enjoy the walk to see who's about. Where is Mark? Is he not helping you now?"

"No son, he works full-time now so I just do the run myself."

"Oh, right. Listen, good seeing you Nigel, but I got to shoot on. If you're round my street next week call in. I would take some bottles off you. We live on the end house near the pigeon club."

"Spot on, son. I will call in next week, sure I will see you then."

And at that Nigel drove off and I walked up the road.

CHAPTER 22

Joe And The Bag

That night in the club we had to close up early as there was a committee meeting, so at 11.30 all the regulars were told to leave. Joe the enforcer made an announcement over the mic.

"Can everyone drink up please and make your way home? We have a bit of business to take care of, thanks very much."

And at that, everyone finished their drinks and left; no one would even question Joe so within ten minutes Billy and I were left with ten other men who were sitting round a table talking.

"Can you get a round of drinks in, Jonny?" Joe asked.

"Yes Joe, no problem."

I went and took the order and poured the drinks. Billy carried them over and I heard Joe say to him after he brought the last drinks over, "Billy, you can head on. Jonny can lock up tonight."

This was becoming the usual situation. I had to stay on till stupid o'clock while Billy went home and these men talked shop.

I sat behind the bar and listened to what was being discussed, and it wasn't long before voices were raised and an argument broke out; Joe threatened a guy called Sam. He said to him, "Your team is out of order. You need to get it sorted, there is two lads under you who are freelancing. It has to stop. People are asking questions about us losing control. I want you to pull them in and make them understand that I'm in control of who does what and when. This fucking robbing has to stop or I will stop it."

"Who the fuck do you think you're talking to? I'm on this road as long as you, Joe. We aren't in school now. You can't dictate what my team do, we are loyal and people need to know we will stop at nothing to raise funds for the cause," Sam replied.

"Fuck your mouth up. I'm still number one – you answer to me and what I say goes. Do you hear me?"

"Oh, I hear you, Joe. I hear you loud and clear."

Tempers were flaring; I genuinely thought fists were going to fly. Just then, a third man got involved.

"Calm down Joe, you're going to give yourself a heart attack. Joe's right, Sam. We are only hurting our own and we don't want our people turning to the U.V.F. for help. That's the last thing we need, a feud on the road."

It was a guy called Norman who spoke up; he was

about 6ft 5 inches tall, of slim build, and grey hair. He was a tough boy – the talk was in his day he had murdered four men in a shootout and had spent the best part of twenty years inside, so when he spoke, you listened, and to be honest if he didn't Joe probably would have pulled a weapon out. It wasn't the first time Joe had lost his rag about robbings going on, and with Sam, the two of them never got on and Norman was spot on. Sam was getting above his station; he and Joe were always at each other's throats. I think Sam wanted to be head of the U.F.F. and Joe knew it.

"So Joe, sit down. You as well, Sam. We don't need this shit, we have more pressing business to talk about," Norman said.

"Jonny, can you get more drinks in?" Joe asked.

"Yes Joe, same again is it?"

"Yes son."

As I poured the drinks I heard Joe say, "We need to put out a statement to the press about this unit from Ardoyne. They have seriously injured one of our men and we'll hit back if it doesn't stop.

"Fuck that. Joe, if they target one of ours we target two of theirs. That's what we should be doing, not putting out fucking statements," Sam replied.

A few of the men agreed with Sam. One of them said, "Sam, you're right. For too long we have just sat back and took this shit. Our statement should be body bags, not fucking words."

"But you have to understand, lads, if we go down that road they will hit back and every one of us are targets. Are yous prepared to put yourselves and your families in that situation?" Joe replied.

"That situation! Fuck me, Joe. We are at war – we are in that situation now. Just look at Jim who's fighting for his life in hospital. Tell that to his family. They fucking shot him leaving his kids at school. So we are already in that position, we need to hit back and straight away," Sam said.

"Ok then Sam, what do you want to do?"

As I brought the drinks over, Sam said to me, "Jonny, can you drive?"

"No Sam, but I want to start."

"Then we can't use you," Sam said.

"I have a boy who we can use," Norman said.

"He has to be clean, no ties with us, Norman," Sam asked.

"He is. He runs jobs for me and has never been picked up. He will do what I ask."

"What's his name and where is he from?" Sam asked.

"He is from Glencairn, his name is Paul. He is a good lad – tough as fuck."

My ears pricked up. I thought to myself, *I bet you that's Paul, Jonty's mate. And yes, he was getting a bad name on the road.*

"Bring him in. I would like to get him more involved, Norman."

"There are three of them, they come as a team."

Yep, it has to be them, I thought.

"What are the names of his mates, Norman?" Sam asked.

"Jonty and Jason. Again, very loyal lads. They will be very willing to get involved and to be honest, we need young blood in and given more responsibility."

I fucking knew it. Oh my god, they are three psychos. if the U.F.F. give them weapons they will go nuts, and to give them a mission would be suicide. They don't have a brain cell between them. If they were in Norman's unit then that's a time bomb ready to go off.

"Bring them in, and I mean tonight, this needs sorted. We have to hit back within days to show them I.R.A. bastards who they are messing with," Sam asked.

Norman lifted his phone and started dialling. I heard him say, "Paul, I want you, Jonty, and Jason down to Heather Street for a meeting. Get a taxi down straight away, it's important."

He hung the phone up and said, "They will be down straight away. You can trust these boys. Whatever I tell them to do, they do it no questions asked."

"Ok Sam, then what's the plan you have?" Joe asked.

"I have a contact and they have given me a free hit on a taxi driver who is a known I.R.A. activist. They want him taken out as he has been credited to two kills and they can't touch him, so they asked could we take him out."

"Fuck me, Sam. Who have you been taking to?"

"You don't need to know, Joe. All you need to

know is that I have it set up for Thursday. I just need the right team to do it."

"What is it then, and is it tight?" Joe asked.

"We get the driver to come to Belfast Castle Country Park where we have a shooter waiting to take him out, then our driver is sitting on the main road where I have been told we have a free passage back to the Shankill."

"How do we get the right driver to go, Sam?" Joe asked.

"We have a spotter on the Antrim road watching the drivers, and when our man is the only driver waiting for a job we book the taxi for a pick and that's how we get him."

"Genius, Sam. Sounds good but are you sure our boys aren't being set up?"

"It's tight, Joe. Trust me, this target is going to be straight forward."

Oh my god. I stood there behind the bar in shock, and just at that, Paul, Jonty, and Jason walked in. Norman stood up.

"Here are my boys now." Norman shook their hands. "Sit down, lads. This is Sam and Joe, we have a job for yous to do."

At that, Joe said to me, "Jonny, just leave the keys behind the bar, I will lock up. I think you have heard enough tonight."

As I lifted my coat, Paul turned to me.

"Alright ball bag, didn't know you worked here."

"Watch your mouth, Paul. Jonny is a good lad so

none of your shit with him," Norman said.

Paul gave me the dirtiest look and just smiled at me.

"I will see you again, Jonny."

I knew what he meant. I fucking hated the three of them. I didn't even answer him, I just walked out the door.

I had only got about ten steps down the street when I heard Joe call me.

"Jonny, come here a minute."

I turned and walked back.

"What is it, Joe?"

"Don't be worrying about them three lads. They have been told you're not to be touched, but what I need you to do is get me my bag back. I need what's in it. Can you get me it for tomorrow night?"

"Yes Joe, not a problem. I will bring it to work tomorrow night, you can collect it any time after six."

"Thanks, son."

He reached into his pocket and handed me an envelope. He said, "Listen, this is for you, and again, nobody knows about our arrangement."

"Thanks Joe, I will see you tomorrow night."

I turned and walked up home.

The following day when my mum and I went to my nanny's for dinner, I went out to the toilet to get the bag. I had brought my kit bag with me to put Joe's bag in it so when I locked the door and reached up to get it I was shocked to find out that Joe's bag was gone.

"Fuck, fuck, fuck," I said.

I pulled the board down and stretched up to see if it had fallen down the back, but no, it wasn't there. I was going to have to ask my nanny if anybody had been out there. I walked into the house, petrified. What was I going to do? If I didn't get Joe his bag I would be in big trouble. Kneecapping trouble. I walked into the kitchen where my mum and nanny were standing.

"Nanny, can I have a word?"

"Yes Jonny, what's wrong, son? Have you lost something?"

She looked at my mum and then my mum looked at me.

"Have you something to say?" my mum asked.

Fuck. They knew. They had found the bag.

"Mum, have you something that doesn't belong to you?"

"Something that doesn't belong to me?" She had raised her voice – she sounded angry.

"Mum, you don't understand. It's not my bag, it belongs to someone else. I was told to hide it."

She hit me with a slap round the head.

"Do you realise what you're getting yourself into, Jonny?"

"Ma, I had no choice, I was told to hide it. I don't even know what's in it but I need to give it back."

"Jonny, you should have told me. I always thought we had no secrets. We could of dealt with it."

Secrets, I thought. *If she only knew the half of it, she would string me up.*

"Where is it, Ma? I have to give it back tonight."

"It's behind your nanny's chair in the corner."

At that, I walked into the living room and reached behind the chair; thank fuck, it was there. Panic over.

"Bring it here, Jonny. I want to see what's in it."

"You can't, Ma. It's stitched shut, I have to bring it back the way it is."

"I'm telling you, son, don't be getting involved with the paramilitaries. It will only end up you going to jail or worse, DEAD."

"I know, Ma. I won't."

I put the bag inside my kit bag and zipped it shut; my mum didn't speak to me the rest of the day. I think she was disgusted at me for having the bag and hiding it in my nanny's.

When I got to work that night I put the kit bag in the store room behind the empty barrels of beer. I made sure Billy couldn't see it, I just carried on getting the bar ready as Sundays were a busy night, especially when it was karaoke night. It always seem to get a good crowd in.

As the night went on there was no sign of Joe. I was starting to panic as I didn't want Billy to find the bag, but we were that busy neither of us got a chance for a break. The night flew in and before I knew it Billy had called for last orders. One of the local singers sang God Save the Queen and the lights were turned on. I looked round the bar but there was no sign of Joe. As I walked round, lifting the glasses and tidying up, I noticed Billy go into the store room. My heart started beating faster; I was praying he wouldn't find Joe's bag. It felt like ages but I couldn't go in I, just waited and waited, and then the door opened and Billy walked out. He had nothing in his hands. *Thank fuck,* I thought. As the last people left Billy turned the lights out.

"Right Jonny, come on, I will drop you home. I'm glad that night's over, I'm bloody knackered. I can't wait to get to my bed and have a good lie in tomorrow. It's been a long weekend."

"Aye Billy, you're right there, I'm shattered. You didn't see Joe come in tonight, did you?"

"Jonny, did you not hear? Joe is lying in the Mater Hospital, he had a massive heart attack late last night driving home. He crashed the car into a neighbour's wall – it doesn't look good for him. It's the talk of the road. I haven't heard any more news so he must be still alive."

"Fuck me, Billy. That's terrible. I hope he is ok."

"Aye son, so do I. I don't fancy that psycho Sam running the road. I don't like him at all, he is a real bad article."

"Yeah Billy, me too. I don't like him either, especially now he has them three muppets Paul, Jonty, and Jason with him. I never got on with them as well, they are real bad news."

As Billy drove me home, he was stopped by a black taxi.

"Billy, did you hear about Joe?" the taxi man asked.

"Aye Jim, I did. He's in the Mater."

"No Billy, he died tonight. It's terrible news."

"Shit, that's terrible. When is the funeral?" Billy asked.

"Not sure, Billy. Most likely Thursday. The word is the road is to be closed, nobody is to open up."

"Thanks for letting me know, Jim. I will check the tele the mara night."

Billy continued on up to my house.

"Frig, Jonny. That's it then. Sam will be put in charge, we are all fuck't now. There will nobody to stop him and his murdering ways now."

I didn't even answer, my thoughts were about the bag and what I was going do with it.

When I got home my mum was sitting waiting for me. She said, "Did you get rid of that bag, Jonny?"

I knew by her tone she was still angry.

"Yes, Ma. I did," I replied, lying through my teeth.

"Never you do that again, do you hear me? Or you're out on the street. I won't have you involved and running with the U.F.F. Do you hear me?"

"Yes Ma. Yes, I hear you."

I went on up to bed; my mind was buzzing. Where was I going to hide the bag? And more important, what the hell was in it?

CHAPTER 23

Mum's The Word

It was all over the news about Joe's death and when I read about him in the Belfast Telegraph he was a real bad man in his day. He had done the lot, from money laundering to racketeering, to murder, but I had liked him. I thought of him as one of the sensible members of the U.F.F. and from what Billy had told me about Sam, we were in for a rough time.

Joe's funeral was to be Thursday and every business on the road was to be closed at 2pm that day as a mark of respect for Joe. When I went down to attend I had never seen as many people in my life, even when I went to the Boxing Day match when Linfield played Glentoran. There were hundreds of people, all standing; the road was black with men in their suits so when it was time for Joe to be carried out of the church the road was filled, and as we walked down the Shankill I stayed near the back. I couldn't even see the hearse which must have been half a mile down the road. When we got to Shankill estate it had stopped. I couldn't see what was going on but what I did see was ten men all dressed in combat gear, and I knew what was going to happen next. The sound of a police helicopter above drowned out the voices of people talking, but it was when three shots were fired in the air, it all kicked off.

Police meat wagons came from everywhere; they tried to get down the road to arrest the men in uniform but they got more than they bargained for. More shots were fired and people were running and screaming everywhere. I ducked behind a wall but every now and again I poked my head up to see what was happening. As I looked up, the police helicopter was that low I could see the pilot. Then I heard a car flying past where I was hiding. I looked up as it screeched to a halt. Four men jumped out of it, all wearing balaclavas; they opened the boot and pulled out the biggest machine gun I had ever seen. They placed it in the middle of the road and one of them lay down on the road as another one loaded it. *Fuck me,* I thought. *They are going to fire this thing.*

I lay down behind the wall and the noise was deafening. A volley of shots were fired and the sirens of the meat wagons and the screeching of tyres were terrible. People were screaming as more shots were fired. The police helicopter flew away and all of a sudden it went quiet. I looked round the corner; the four men were standing there just watching up the road. I looked round and there wasn't a peeler in sight. The four of them calmly just packed the gun away and got into the car and drove off.

I stood up to see if anyone was hurt. A man with a

loud speaker asked everyone to calm down and show respect for Joe.

Respect? I thought. *Fuck me. Respect? Is he serious?*

Amazingly nobody was killed that day, but it was obvious that it had been pre-planned and the U.F.F. were having a show of strength to let the world know they run the road and will stop at nothing to have the power.

*

That night in the club it was full of U.F.F. members, and if only they knew I had Joe's bag, I would be a dead man, but there was no way I was handing it over. I knew nobody now knew I had it and to be honest it was now eating me up inside what was in it.

As the night went on and the drunker the men got, there were a few fights that broke out. At one stage there were four men knocking the shit clean out of each other. Nobody stopped it until it was over and it shocked the shit clean out of me, as when it had stopped what was left of the men got up and walked to the bar. I stood there, dumbfounded, just looking at them, blood running out of them. One of them said, "Fuck's sake, will you go and pour a drink and get a couple of cloths? We need to get cleaned up."

I had never poured four vodkas as quick. They didn't even want a mixer, the four of them stood there and just downed the glasses. Afterwards they shook hands and I handed each of them a cloth and they walked away, wiping their faces.

It was a really late night. It must have went on till three in the morning. I was absolutely shattered and just wanted to go home, with my bag of course.

Billy told me that I could shoot on and that was my cue. Into the back store room and there behind the empty barrels was my bag. I lifted it out and put my coat on. As I walked back out to the bar, Billy was standing with Big Sam and Norman, talking about the events of the day and I overheard big Sam say, "Well that's the sending off Joe would of wanted, to strike fear back into them peelers. They are going to have to learn not to mess with us and that the lower Shankill is a no-go area."

"Aye, you're right, Sam. We will have to organise that hit we discussed. The I.R.A. bastards are going to have to be taught a lesson," Norman replied.

"Yes Norman, we will have a full meeting next week sometime and get it sorted."

As I looked over, Billy said to me, "Is that you away, Jonny?"

"Yes Billy, it is. I will see you tomorrow night."

"Jonny, we aren't opening tomorrow night. Take the night off, I will see you Saturday."

"Spot on, Billy."

I nodded to Big Sam and Norman and proceeded to walk out the door.

As I walked up home the sound of police sirens was still in the air and the police helicopter was still flying about. It looked like it was over Glencairn and it had a search light on, as the big beam of light was fixated round about that direction. I kept my head down; there were still some men walking about. I had the bag over my shoulder and it was quite heavy. It was doing my crust in wanting to open it but I had to pick my time and place.

As I walked up to the front door of my house I could see my ma's bedroom light on, so it was as quietly as I could be that I put my key in the door and opened it up. I closed it again behind me as quietly as I could and started the slow walk up the stairs, putting my feet only on the boards that didn't creak. I was a real expert at this now, many a night coming home not wanting to wake my ma. As I got to the top of the stairs I stopped and listened. No movement – great. Into my bedroom and I closed the door behind me. Shit, I heard my ma get out of bed.

"Jonny, come here son."

I stashed the bag under my bed and walked over and opened her door.

"Yes Ma, what is it?"

"Just checking you're ok, love. It's all over the news about today, there is trouble all over Belfast."

"Aye, Ma. I was in the bar all night, I didn't see any of it."

"Jonny, this road is getting worse. Promise me you're not in any trouble. I worry myself sick about you, son. You should get yourself out of here, there's nothing left but misery."

"Ma, stop talking like that. I'm not that stupid and I'm not leaving you. We will be fine."

"I hope you're right, son. Away into bed, I will see you in the morning."

"Ok Ma, night-night."

I closed her door and went into my bedroom; I got undressed and into bed. I lay there just listening the helicopter; it was away in the distance and the sirens had stopped as well. My mind was buzzing, I just wanted to rip that bag open and see what was in it, and the sound of my ma's snoring was my cue. I got out of bed and pulled open my curtains. The light from the street light was enough for me to see under my bed. I lifted the bag out and set it on my bed. I went into my drawer and lifted out an aul pen knife I had, and cut the stitching round the zip.

I took a second and said softly, "Well, here goes nothing."

I slowly zipped the bag open and opened it up wide. I was breathless, my heart was pounding. I reached in and pulled out two bundles of notes, then another two and another two. I set them on my bed. I had never seen as much money. I examined them closer. All twenty pound notes. *Fuck, there must be thousands of pounds here.* I looked into the bag and out I took two hand guns and four boxes of bullets. There must have been over a hundred rounds of ammo there and as I looked into the bag again I lifted out a passport that was Joe's and one more bundle of ten pound notes.

I sat there on the edge of my bed and thought to myself, *Holy fuck, this was Joe's stash. His get-out money and his guns.* I must have sat for a good twenty minutes pondering what to do. Do I hand it back? Do I hand it in to the peelers? Do I tell my ma? I told myself that I would sleep on it and deal with it tomorrow, and that's what I did.

The next morning I must have slept in till after

lunch; the events of the previous day had caught up with me and when I opened my eyes all I could think of was the money and what was I going to do.

I went downstairs and my mum was in the kitchen.

"Alright, so would you like some breakfast? I mean, lunch," she asked as she looked up to the clock.

"Yeah Ma, that would be lovely, I'm starving."

"A fry, ok then."

"Brill, Ma."

As I stood in our kitchen watching my ma cook over that dingy cooker, I had never noticed how little we had. I turned and looked round the living room. The suite had seen better days and the carpet was done as well. My heart dropped. My ma has had nothing but heartache her whole life, and that's when I decided to keep the money and give my ma a better life and a nicer house to live in.

"Jonny, here's your lunch, son."

I turned and my ma had a big fry for me. My mouth watered as I sat at the table and got stuck into it – it was beaut.

"For goodness' sake, Jonny. Come up for air," my ma said.

I stopped eating. "I know, Ma. It's lovely... Ma, I have been putting money away, would you like to go out today? My treat?"

"For what, Jonny?"

"Ma, our wee house could do with being done up and I want to pay to get it done." I thought to myself,

Well, Joe is paying, and I smiled at her.

"Jonny, I would love to get it done up, that would be brilliant son, but I don't want you spending your money, you work too hard for it."

"Ma, if I can't spend it on you, who can I spend it on?"

"Only if you're sure, son."

I knew by looking at her she was really excited; she had a smile on her face I hadn't seen in a while.

"Right, it's settled then. We are going shopping."

After I got ready I went into Joe's bag and counted out 200 quid. My mum and I went down the road to pick wallpaper out of Noblets; we picked some paint as well. On the way back up in the taxi I got him to stop outside the carpet shop. When we went in, the man behind the desk said, "Good afternoon, can I help you with anything?"

I looked at him hard. I knew his face; he was one of the men that sat in the committee meetings – he looked at me.

"Awk, alright Jonny? How's it going, son?"

"Alright, just out to get a bit of carpet for our house."

"Well you're in the right place then. Have you any idea of your sizes?"

Me and my ma looked at each other.

"No, we don't. I wouldn't know how to measure it."

"Don't worry Jonny, just pick what you need and I

will nip up and get the sizes for you. Where is it for?"

"The living room and the stairs, and if you do me a good deal could you do the two bedrooms as well?"

"Course I can, Jonny. Listen, we have a deal on at the minute. Five rooms for 200 quid, fitted as well, and if you want a bit of vinyl that would be grand."

"That's perfect, we will go for that."

My ma turned to me.

"Jonny, that's too much. Just the living room will do."

"No Ma, we are getting the house done."

I turned to the man and said, "You wouldn't happen to know a painter and decorator, would you?"

"Yes son, my brother-in-law does a bit of that. I will give you his number."

"Brilliant, could you give him a ring now for us? I would want him to start straight away if that suits him."

"Yep, no worries." He lifted the phone and called him; his name was Trevor and he could start the next day. I gave him our address and he was to call that night to see what needed to be done.

"Right, what carpet do you need? If you come over here I will show you the ones that's in the offer."

"Jonny, are you sure you want to do this, son? It's a lot of money."

"Yes Ma, you just need to worry about picking your colours."

My ma gave me a big hug. I felt great, I didn't

realise that spending money was so much fun. As we walked over to the back of the shop there were six different carpets to choose from. My ma was like a child in a sweet shop: 'This one for here, that one for there, and oh yes, that vinyl would be lovely in the kitchen and the bathroom.'

When she had picked all the rooms we lifted our paint and paper and got a taxi up the road.

"Could you stop here, mister?" I asked the taxi man.

"Where are we going now, Jonny?" my mum asked.

"Into the electric shop, we need a new cooker."

"Indeed we don't, the one I have works perfect."

"No, Ma. We are getting a new one. That one we have you got out of the second hand shop and you deserve a nice new one."

As we walked into the electric shop my ma said to me, "Jonny, where did you get the money from? Did you get a bet up or something?"

"No, Ma. I told you, I have been saving and Billy looks after me, so stop worrying about the money."

"Ok son, I can't thank you enough. It's far too much."

We looked round the shop and my ma picked the only one on offer, which didn't surprise me – she loved a bargain.

The woman behind the counter said, "That's a good choice, that's a crack'n wee cooker. I have one myself – you couldn't beat it for the money."

If only my ma knew I was sitting on thousands, she could have had the top of the range one, but she was so happy at getting the one she picked.

"Do you need it delivered?"

"Yes we do, can you deliver it in a couple of weeks as we are decorating first?"

"Yes love, that's not a problem. Do you want to pay a deposit and come down and pay the rest when you want it dropped up?"

"That's perfect," I said, and I handed her twenty quid.

Off we went again and it was only a short walk up to the next row of shops, where I got my ma to choose a nice lamp, mirror, and a tall vase with fancy artificial flowers which we had to leave to get picked up the next day as I was hung carrying the paint, and my ma as well with the wallpaper.

That night I sent my ma to the bingo after the man had called about doing the decorating, so when she left to go I was straight into my bag to count the money. I was busting to know how much there actually was. It took me about an hour and when I finished counting my fingers were sore but I had the guts of 32,000 pounds – an absolute fortune, but the problem I faced now was where to hide it that was safe. I sat there in my bedroom and wracked my brain, but I decided the best place was in the loft, and that's where it went. I kept about 500 down to cover the house getting done and a few quid for my pocket.

That Saturday I met Karen in Belfast. I had phoned her in the morning to arrange to go for lunch; it had been a few days since I last had seen her and when I did I was so glad to meet with her again. She was really good fun to be with. As we walked round town we chatted about what was going on in our lives and I was really keen to hear about what she had been up to, and to be honest I could have let her talk all day – she was good fun. We went for lunch in Hi Park Centre. There was a really good sandwich bar in there and you got a free refill for tea or coffee. As we sat chatting she said to me, "Have you ever thought about getting your driving licence, Jonny?"

"I have but have never got round to it, but I'm going to start driving lessons soon."

That sparked an idea in my head. I really wanted a wee motor of my own, then I could meet Karen anytime I wanted.

"You really should, Jonny. It would mean we could meet more often."

Music to my ears. It was settled, I was going to learn to drive and get a motor.

We walked round the shops in Hi Park, and I spotted a lovely suite of furniture that would do our wee living room just perfect, and when I looked at the price tag it read £350 – a pure bargain. I said to the guy that was serving, "I would take that suite if you can deliver it up the Shankill."

"No problem, son. It's the last one, so that's why it's that price."

"Yeah, no worries. Could you hold onto it for me for a couple of weeks if I leave you a deposit?"

"Certainly son, can you give me fifty quid?"

I reached into my pocket and pulled out my money. I lifted out three twenty pound notes.

"Here, take the sixty, I will come down Monday

week and pay you the rest and arrange for you to drop it off."

"Spot on, son. Hold on till I give you a receipt."

As we stood there Karen said to me, "Why are you buying a suite, Jonny?"

"My ma's getting the house done up and it would be a nice surprise for her when it arrives."

She smiled at me, and as the man handed me the docket she took my hand and we walked off.

We dandered through town, holding hands. Karen had to get her bus home as she was heading out that night with her mates. Unfortunately I had to work as usual so I gave her a kiss and waved her goodbye.

CHAPTER 24

My Fiesta Xr2

As I walked back up the Shankill my mind was focused on learning to drive. I really wanted this now but hadn't a clue how to go about it, so that night at work I got talking to Billy.

"Billy, if I wanted to learn to drive how would I go about it?"

"You need to apply for your provisional driving licence, son, which takes a bit of time."

"Crap," I replied.

"Why? What's the rush, son? If you really want to learn I have a mate works for the D.V.L.A. I could probably have your licence through in a week, just get me two photos and I will do the rest, and I know a guy who will have you put through your test in about ten days. It will cost you a couple of hundred quid but you would be good to go."

"That's perfect, Billy. I will get you photos on Monday and will get you the money as well."

"No worries, son. Now get the rest of the bar stocked up before the headers arrive. We are having a fundraiser tonight so it will be busy."

I was so excited. I was going to get my licence. "No worries, Billy. Will do."

I stocked that bar in about twenty minutes so time for a wee pint before opening.

Billy wasn't joking – we were packed out that night. I had never seen as much drink drank in all the time I had worked there. It was a fund raiser for the Prody boys flute band and the comedian they had on was brilliant. He was hilarious, people were actually crying at his jokes, and then a band came on – three girls and a fella, and the girls were real lookers; short skirts, the whole shabang, and they were actually very good so it was no surprise it was a real good night. I heard one of the men at the end say that they had raised two grand, which got a big cheer from the crowd.

We got the last of them out about 2am and got locked up. Billy drove me up home, which was glad of, 'cause my feet were killing me. I was glad to get to my bed.

I must have slept till lunchtime but when I got up my mum wasn't in. I was a bit worried but with the smell of a chicken cooking in the oven, I knew she wasn't too far. The smell was making me hungry. I thought to myself, *Winner, winner, chicken dinner*, but had to settle for a bowl of cornflakes as I couldn't be annoyed to make anything else. I sat on our sofa and watched the TV; the football was on form.

Yesterday's games and I had just timed it well – Man U against Newcastle, great game, and when I looked round the Man U team it reminded me of my Milk Cup, as there, lining up for the Red Devils, were the same players that I had seen up in Coleraine back when I was sixteen. *Fuck me,* I thought. *These guys are superstars now. If only I could of got further I might have been on that team.*

Man U beat Newcastle 3-0 and Beckham scored one of his trademark free kicks. He really was some player.

As I put my bowl in the sink my ma came through the front door.

"Hiya Ma, where have you been?"

"I had to nip out to the shop, son, to get some spuds."

"Here Ma, Billy is organising for me to get driving. Isn't that brilliant?"

"Aye son, is he paying for it?"

I sort of hesitated. "Aye Ma, he is. It's so I can go and pick up stock from the cash and carry."

"That's super, son."

I hated lying to my ma but I was getting good at it. I sat back down on the sofa and lifted last night's tele, and went straight to the used cars for sale section. There was every car you could think of from, Minis to BMWs, but my focus was one that was for sale in Bangor – a white Ford Fiesta 1.4 CR2 1996. Only five years old and low mileage, but it was 1,900 quid. Then again, I was well-heeled so the only problem I would have is another lie to my ma, so I ripped the ad out and said to her, "Ma, I have to nip out for a while. I will be back for my dinner."

"Alright son, see you later."

I walked onto the Shankill and straight to the pay phone. I lifted the ad out of my pocket and dialled the number. It was a guy called William who was selling it – he said that his daughter didn't like it as it was too fast. Music to my ears. *The faster the better,* I thought.

"Whereabouts in Bangor do you live?" I asked.

He replied, "Kilcoole estate," and gave me his address. My only problem now was how to get down. I was going to have to ask Billy, but how was I going to explain where the money was coming from to pay for it?

I went round in my head all day until work that night, when I built up the courage up to ask Billy.

I waited for a quiet part of the night and I said to Billy, "Billy, can I ask you something?"

"Fuck, Jonny. The last time you said that it was a trip to the doctors. Please tell me it's not an itch again?"

I laughed. "No, Billy, it's not an itch. Is there any chance I could borrow some money to buy a car?"

Billy stood there; it felt like absolute ages before he replied, "Aye, Jonny. How much do you need?"

"The car is £1,800 but I have saved a bit of money. I would need 1,200 if you could manage that?"

"Yes Jonny, that's not a problem. How do you mean to pay me back?"

"Would you take a hundred a month? I could afford to give you that."

"No worries, son. When do you need it for?"

"Well that's the thing. Can you take me down to see it? You know more about motors than I ever will."

"Yes son, that's fine. Is tomorrow morning ok?"

"Perfect Billy, about eleven ok?"

"Yes son, that's fine. I will pick you up and we will get them photos as well, when we are out."

I stood the rest of the night behind the bar with the biggest cheezer you have ever seen. Even one of the punters said, "Jonny, you look not wise in the head with that stupid grin on your face. You look like the cat that has got the cream."

"Aye mate, you're right. The cat I am." I just kept smiling.

The next morning I got up early. My ma was already away out to her wee cleaning job so I got up into the loft to get some money. I lifted out a bundle of twenties and brought it into my room. I counted out 1,400 quid, put the rest under my mattress, and got myself ready to meet Billy and go and buy my first car. I was buzzing; every time I looked at the clock it seemed to have stopped. It felt like two days had passed. By the time 11 o'clock came I was like a cat on a hot tin roof, pacing the floors, looking out the front door, waiting for Billy. And to top it off he didn't turn up till ten past. I just couldn't hide my excitement. When I got into the car Billy said to me, "Well Jonny, looking forward to go down and see this motor?"

"Aye Billy, I couldn't sleep all night. Can't wait to buy it."

"Hold fire, son. Don't be too eager – it might be a bundle of crap, and even if it's a wee cracker we will try and get a few quid off, so don't be showing the guy down here that you have bought it even before you take it for a spin."

"I know, Billy, but I really want it."

"I remember my first car, son. It's the best feeling in the world. We will go and get your photos done; I have already spoken with my mate in the D.V.L.A. and he is going to meet us in town. He reckons he will have your provisional through by next week."

"Brilliant Billy, and what about your brother-in-law? Is he going to take me on lessons?"

"Yep, all sorted. Soon as you get your provisional he's taking you out, but he is looking for his money up front, son."

I reached into my pocket and lifted my money out and counted Billy 200 quid.

"There you go, Billy. Give him that and you reckon about ten days and I will be ready for my test?"

"Aye Jonny, soon as he gets you out he will make sure you're ready. He's taking you out twice a day every day so it won't take long at all."

"Brilliant Billy, thanks mate."

We drove down the road and stopped at one of the chemists to get my photos done, and then down into town where Billy had arranged to meet his mate to apply for my provisional driving licence. I paid the guy twenty quid for the application and he got me to fill a form in, and off we went to Bangor to get my car.

It took us about thirty minutes to get down to

Bangor; I thought at one stage Billy was slowing down to make sure he got every bloody red light. I swear a guy on a bike overtook us at one stage. I was chomping at the bit, but when we eventually got to Kilcoole estate we pulled into one of the streets and there she was, gleaming bright white, cracking spoiler and body kit on it – she was a smasher. As we pulled up behind it I was out of the car even before it had stopped and over to get a good look at it. Billy came over and stood beside me.

"Calm down, Jonny. Remember we want to try and knock a few quid off."

"I know, Billy, but what do you think?"

Just at that, William came out and walked over to us, holding the keys.

"Alright lads." He looked at me. "I take it you're Jonny?"

"Yes I am." I put my hand out and shook William's.

"This is Billy, my boss."

Billy and William shook hands.

"Can you tell me a wee bit about the car and why you're selling her?" Billy asked.

"Yes, the car I bought for my daughter. She has had it a year now but to be honest she never liked it, she said it was too fast and thought that when she drove it that everyone was looking at her. She is a quiet girl and didn't like the attention so I have got her that wee Mini over there and she loves it, so I'm getting rid of this one now as it's not needed."

"Oh right, can we get a look inside and take it for a spin?" Billy asked.

"Yes, not a problem. Here's the keys but can you leave your keys of your car? Don't take it the wrong way, I don't trust anyone when it comes to business."

"Yes, that's no worries. I feel the same way so I know where you're coming from, William," Billy replied, and he handed William his keys.

"Thanks Billy, take as long as you need," William replied and walked back over to his house.

Billy opened the car and said, "Well get in, Jonny, and we will take it for a spin."

I opened up the passenger door and got in. It was lovely – pure class. It was like a brand new motor, even had that new car smell in it. Billy started it up and it purred like a lion; he gave it a couple of revs and off we went. We drove out onto the carriageway and Billy said, "Let's see what this thing can do now."

He dropped it down a gear and I swear I got whiplash as he floored it. I looked over. Fifty... sixty... then seventy miles an hour. This thing could shift.

"Fuck's sake, Billy, slow down. You're gonna get a ticket if the peelers get you."

"Don't worry, Jonny. Want to give it a good run to do a few checks on it."

We pulled off the next turning and pulled into a street and stopped.

"Right, let's have a look at the engine, Jonny."

As Billy reached down to open the bonnet I got out of the car. I walked to the front of the motor and Billy opened up the bonnet.

"She looks clean enough, Jonny," Billy said.

Billy then opened the oil filler cap and looked at it.

"Why are you looking at that, Billy?"

"To check the head gasket Jonny, but it's fine."

He then got down and looked under the car.

"What are you doing now, Billy?" I asked.

"It's fine, Jonny. No oil about it. It's definitely the car for you, son. It's a clean wee motor."

I smiled and Billy closed the bonnet. We both got in again and drove it back to William's house.

"Now before we talk money, I will do the talking, Jonny. See if we can get a few quid off."

"Ok Billy, no worries."

We both got out and William came walking over.

"Well what do you think, do you like it, Jonny?"

"I will take it," I said, as Billy just stood there and looked at me.

He just laughed and said, "Thought we were gonna try and bargain William down, you header."

"I know, Billy, but I really want it and it's a fair price as it is. But I need a favour off you, William, before I buy it."

"What is it, Jonny?" William asked.

"I see you have a garage there at the side of your house. If I buy the motor could you keep it in there until I pass my test in two weeks?"

"Yes, that's not a problem."

"Ok then, I will take her." I reached into my pocket. "Can I give you this 500 quid as a deposit and pay you the rest when I come to pick it up?"

"Yep, that's fine."

William shook my hand and the deal was done.

As Billy and I drove home, we had just got out of Kilcoole estate when he said to me, "You're a smooth operator, Jonny. I must say you nailed him to the fence there with that hard bargaining you done."

I laughed.

"I know, Billy, but I just fell in love with the car and had to have it."

Billy laughed.

"I know how it goes, son. I think you got a good car there. Now you have to get your test and there will be no looking at you. The girls will be chasing after you all over the Shankill in that babe magnet."

"Aye Billy, it's a nice motor."

Billy dropped me off home and I couldn't wait to tell my ma the news. As I walked in through the front door my ma was sitting watching the telly.

"Alright Ma, do you want to know where I was?"

"Where, Jonny?"

"Just bought myself a car and I pick it up in a couple of weeks when I get my driving licence."

She jumped straight up.

"You have done what?"

"Stop panicking, Billy has lent me the money. I'm paying him back out of my wages and his mate is teaching how to drive, so I'm sorted. Ma, the car is lovely. It's white and really sporty. I can't wait to get it."

"Awk I'm pleased for you, son. You are really doing well for yourself. You're growing up too fast. Before I know it you will be getting married and have kids of your own."

"No chance, Ma. Too much partying to do before I settle down."

We both laughed and I said, "Do you fancy a brew, Ma?"

"What, are you not feeling well? My Jonny offering to make tea?"

"Aye Ma, think I'm burning a temperature."

She laughed. I went and made us a wee cuppa and brought in a couple of chocolate biscuits.

Life was great. I couldn't wait to get driving. The next few days dragged in but on Friday when I got into work Billy had a smirk on his face.

"Alright Jonny, I have something for you."

"What is it, Billy? Please tell me the toilets aren't blocked. I'm not in the mood to go up to my elbows in crap again."

Billy laughed.

"No son, I got your provisional licence back from my mate. You're good to start your lessons. My mate will pick you up in the morning for 10 o'clock for your first lesson. You call him Derek."

"Fuck, that's weaker, Billy. How long do you think it will take?"

"Usually an hour a lesson," Billy said with a laugh.

"No, Billy, to get my full licence."

"I'm only winding you up. He said he should have you through in no more than ten days, but he needs to get you out in his car before he will know."

"Perfect Billy, looking forward to it."

The next morning I was up with the birds waiting for Derek to come, and bang on 10 o'clock, a knock came to the door. I answered it and this strange-looking we man with the worst wig I have ever seen was standing in the street in front of a nice Fiesta with a learner's sign on the roof. I knew then it was Derek.

"Hello," he said in what I think was a Scottish accent.

"You must be Jonny. I'm Derek, Billy's mate. I'm here to teach you how to drive."

I had to strain my ears – I couldn't make out a word he was saying. I heard 'Derek' and 'drive', but the rest was just sounds. I thought to myself, *This is going to be awkward.* I couldn't take my eyes off his wig. I swear it looked like roadkill and his black-framed glasses weren't really a good look either, but suppose beggars couldn't be choosers.

"Yes, I'm Jonny, and thanks for doing this. Did Billy give you the money?"

"Yes he did. He told me you want the quick package, is that right?"

Again, the words I heard were 'yes' and 'quick'.

"Yep, as quick as you can get me through."

Fuck, I thought. *I hope he's talking about getting me through my test.* This really was going to be a challenge.

"Right, well then let's get started." And Derek

pointed to the car.

It's as well I was fluent in sign language as the old ears couldn't hear a whole sentence Derek was saying. I walked over to the driver's side and got in. Derek got into the passenger side and closed the door, then he lifted a clipboard and started talking and pointing at diagrams and pointing to the pedals on the floor.

I deciphered the code he was talking and worked out the accelerator, the clutch, and the brake. Derek then nodded and I nodded back. He then said, "Start her up, lad, and let's get going." I thought he said to rev the fuck clean out of it as I turned the ignition on but apparently not, as Derek started shouting, "Take your foot off the accelerator!"

As the engine stopped screaming I concentrated really hard and listened to Derek.

"Now listen lad, driving isn't complicated, it is people who make it hard. Everything you do, take your time and concentrate on what I'm trying to teach you." He said it really slowly and it felt like I was back in school and about five years old.

"That's easy for you to say, Derek. I'm really nervous."

"You will be fine, just take your time and do everything slowly. Now put the clutch in and put it into first gear, then look at your mirrors before moving off."

Again, didn't really take much out of that conversation so I just put it in first gear, looked at my mirror, indicated, and off we went. Well, sort of off we went. The car must have had kangaroo petrol cause the fucking thing hopped and jumped down my street, but it calmed down when I turned out onto Tennett Street and I was driving ok.

"That's not bad, son. You have the basics, just take your time and do everything slowly."

I did my best to listen to Derek but he didn't make it easy with his foreign language. For a solid hour we drove round the Shankill, up and down all the wee streets until I was used to stopping and starting.

Derek dropped me off back home and told me he would be back at four for another lesson, so I just lazed about the house waiting to get back on the road again.

This was the same format for a solid week, and I was now able to understand Derek when he spoke, but it was the following Wednesday when Derek told me that he had put in for my test and it was the Friday morning. This was just before he was getting me to do an emergency stop.

We were driving in and around the Shankill estate when Derek got me to parallel park in between two parked cars. It was a gift – I had that bit nailed on. As I put the handbrake on Derek said to me, "Right son, we are going to teach you the right way to control an emergency stop. When we drive off again you will see me hit the dashboard with my clipboard. When that happens you need to get on with the anchors as fast as you can. Just imagine a child has run out in front of you and you have to get stopped."

"Ok Derek, no worries. I can do that," I replied.

So off we went. We got about 100 yards up the street when I saw out of the corner of my eye, Derek looking at his rear-view mirror, and he lifted his hand with the clipboard in it. That was my cue. Well, I thought it was. I slammed the brakes on so hard Derek flew forward. His wig ended up on the dashboard and to be honest if he hadn't been wearing his seatbelt he would have been out through the front windscreen and kissing the road.

"Fuck me, Jonny. I hadn't hit the dashboard with the clipboard yet." As he leant forward and lifted his wig and put it back on his head backwards, I may add I just looked at him and burst out laughing.

"What are you laughing at? Is it my wig?" he asked.

The tears were coming down my cheeks. I couldn't answer him for laughing.

"It's not that bloody funny. I don't like being bald and I think it doesn't look too bad."

I composed myself.

"It's not, Derek, but you have the bloody thing on back to front."

As Derek looked in the mirror, he laughed.

"Fuck, you're right son." And he turned it round.

As we sat there in the car we both had a quare laugh at it and Derek said to me, "I will tell you what, Jonny, that was a quare stop you made and you didn't even stall the car. Well done, son. You're ready for your test."

"Thanks Derek, I hope I get it first time."

"You will, son. You're a good wee driver. Just lay off the heavy right foot and don't go too fast and you will be grand."

"Thanks Derek, will do."

Derek dropped me back home and I had a couple more lessons before my test on Friday.

Friday arrived and Derek picked me up and took me to the test centre. We went over a few things and Derek went over and spoke to the driving test instructor. He looked about 6ft 6 inches tall, built like a jockey's whip and with bright ginger hair. He walked over and got into the passenger side. When he closed the door he said to me, "Listen son, I'm a very good friend of Derek's. You have no need to worry about this test, you have passed already. We just need to disappear for half an hour to make it look like I'm testing you."

I was dumbstruck.

"Ok then," I replied. "Where would you like me to drive to?"

"There is a nice wee coffee shop down the road a bit. Pull into it and we will get a cuppa. So away you go, son."

I was in shock; I think it would have been easier just to get tested but it is what it is, and off we went.

I parked the car outside the coffee shop and asked the man, "How do you like your coffee, mister?"

"Like my women, son. Large and sweet."

I laughed. I should introduce him to Orange Lil – he would love her.

"No worries, back in a minute."

And I got out and went into the café. When I returned to the car we just sat there and drank our coffee. We sat and chatted and I told him about my car and how I couldn't wait to get driving it. He told me about his motor and how he loved it but wife was trying to get him to change it to a seven-seater for more room, but he was digging his heels in. He said, "How the hell can you go from a Toyota Supra 3.0 super charge to a bloody minibus? My street cred would be zero. She has no chance of getting me to change my motor."

I just laughed and finished my coffee.

"Will we head back now, son?"

"Yeah, that was tough going," I said and laughed.

As we drove back up to the test centre he asked me to pull over to where Derek was sitting on a wall and he wound his window down.

"Where did you get this one from, Derek? He didn't even buy me a bun with my coffee."

Derek replied, "You're a bloody geg, Jim. He's a good friend of the family," and winked.

"Oh right, that's ok then."

He turned to me.

"Right, ok Jonny, that's you sorted. Just sign here and your licence will be out with you in five days, but you're good to start driving soon as you get your insurance sorted."

"Thanks Jim, that's brilliant. Thanks again, I'm chuffed to bits."

"No worries lad, just be careful out on them roads. There is some head cases out there with dodgy wigs." He laughed and looked round at Derek.

"You takin' the piss again, Jim?"

"No Derek, just telling the lad to drive carefully."

"Aye, I know, Jim. You're a laugh a minute."

In the next couple of days I got my insurance and most important, Billy took me down to Bangor and I picked up my XR2. Driving home in my car, I was over the moon. I had the music blasting and had the window down and just was a pure poser. It was great to have the freedom of being able to go anywhere without relying on a taxi or bus, but most important, when I arranged to meet Karen, the look on her face when I turned up at her door to pick her up was priceless. She loved the motor. It was just weeker driving round with Karen sitting beside me. We even took a wee trip down to Newcastle, and when we pulled up in Donard cark park, all the boy racers were there in their sporty motors, but I had mine gleaming, and it was just class as they all turned their heads to see my motor.

CHAPTER 25

The Hit

A few days later when I was working in the club, the usual men stayed on late for their committee meeting. Big Sam headed the table along with five others and his henchmen as well – Jonty, Jason, and Paul, who were now well established in the U.F.F. as a beating squad, so I kept my head down and just poured the drinks.

Big Sam asked Billy to go on home and told me to stay on to lock up, so it was the usual 'hear no evil, see no evil'. It was getting late when I heard Sam say, "Right, so it's set. Paul, you are the driver, Jason, you are the spotter, and Jonty, you have to take him out. This bastard is an I.R.A. activist and will be a big scalp if we can take him out. Jonty, you will be in place up in Belfast Castle. Paul, you will be parked just out on the road facing down the Antrim road, and Jason, you will be in place just opposite the taxi depo. When our man is the only car outside we make the call for a pick up to come to Belfast Castle, where Jonty, you take him out. It's set for this Thursday, everyone to meet here for 6pm. That's when his shift starts so I want us all to be in place at 7pm."

"What about the getaway? Is it going to be safe, Sam?" Jonty asked.

"Everything will be in place. I have got police scanners so we can monitor police conversations, and the gun will be clean so you will have no worries, son. The only thing you need to worry about is making sure you nut this bastard."

"No problem, Sam. That won't be a problem. Just get him there and I will take him out."

Just at that, the front door was pushed open and the police came rushing in.

"Nobody move! Get your hands on the table where I can see them."

An extremely large policeman pointing his gun at Sam was really aggressive.

"I can't see your fucking hands, Sam. Get them on the table. This is a raid so nobody move."

Holy fuck, I was petrified. With all these men from the U.F.F. and me being in the same room, I was going to be in the same boat. Sam started shouting at the police, "Yous don't have anything on me so do what you want? You got fuck all, yous are a pack of black bastards with nothing better to do, so work away."

"Where is the owner of the bar?" he asked as he looked at me.

"Billy went home early but I will ring him if you want."

"Yes, get him here. We are going to search the place so he needs to be here."

I went to the phone behind the bar and rang Billy and told him the score. He said he would be there in twenty minutes, so I told the peeler and he said, "I can't wait twenty minutes – we go now." He turned to another peeler dressed in boiler suit and said, "Right, let's go. You start behind the bar, the rest of you search these men starting with him."

He pointed to Sam. He made all the men stand against a wall with their backs to the bar, and his officers proceeded to search them. He said to me, "You as well. Get over here."

As I walked over to where Sam and the others were being searched I noticed the peeler behind the bar had a bag with him. I thought that this was really strange. What was he doing with a bag? The big peeler saw that I had seen his officer with the bag, and he grabbed my shirt.

"Get the fuck over here now." And he shoved me towards the wall where another peeler started searching me. He said to me, "Have you anything on you I need to know about?"

"No, mister, I don't. I just work here," I replied.

He kept patting me down but found nothing; he turned me round and told me to go and sit in the corner. I noticed that the peeler that was behind the bar wasn't there anymore, he was standing talking with the big peeler. He was nodding. Just at that, Billy came through the front door.

"What the fuck are yous doing in my bar? Have you got a search warrant? Tell me you do."

"Well we are waiting for one. It should have been here," the big peeler replied.

"At this time of night? I don't think so. Get your men and get the fuck out of my bar before I report you for trespassing."

"We are searching for weapons and these men are known to us, so we have every right to be here," he said as he pointed over to Sam.

"These men are committee members of a local football team and the only right you have is fucking right turn, so get the fuck out of here now."

I had never seen Billy be so aggressive before, but he gave them a good earful and told them to leave.

As the peelers left, Billy followed them out. I heard him pull the shutter down and he returned to the bar.

"Fuck'n bastards, they are." He looked at me.

"Jonny, where did they search?"

"They just searched all of us. Oh, hold on. There was one of them behind the bar with a bag."

Billy just stood there and put one finger over his lips.

"Quiet lads, nobody say anything."

Billy went behind the bar and started looking. I heard him move glasses and then I heard him say, "Got ya, you wee fucker."

He stood up, holding a small black box with a couple of wires coming from it. It was about the size of a lighter and I hadn't got a clue what it was.

Billy set it on the bar and looked over at Sam and

the other men, who were all sat round the table.

"Sam, continue your meeting about the football club, mate."

He pointed to the black box and shook his head.

"So, who needs a drink?" Billy asked as he searched round the bar again.

The men in turn replied, giving their orders for drinks. Billy went into the back store room and came out with a hammer. He walked over to the bar where the black box was and beat the shit clean out of it. He was swearing as he hit it.

"Fuck'n bastards trying to listen in on us. Yous are a pack of dirty cunts!" He smashed it to pieces.

Billy stopped with the hammer and said, "That's better, they won't hear anything now, the black bastards."

All the men laughed and Sam said, "How did you know, Billy?"

"The peeler in the boiler suit isn't a normal peeler. The raid was a set-up so he could plant this bug." And Billy lifted the remains of the black box and threw it in the fire, where it melted and burst into flames.

"Well done, Billy. That saved a lot of grief. Now, on with the business in hand," Sam replied.

"Right, so we are set for Thursday. Meet here for 6pm. Jonny, I want you here as well."

As Sam looked over at me, so did Jonty, Jason, and Paul.

"Sam, I'm not speaking out of turn but what the

fuck is he to be here for?" Jonty asked.

"You are speaking out of turn if I want him to be here, ok!"

"Ok Sam, I'm only asking. No need to bite my fucking head off."

Just at that, Sam jumped up and hit Jonty with a smack on the jaw. His chair fell backwards and two other men jumped up to restrain Sam.

"Don't fucking speak to me like that. I will put one in your head, speaking to me like that, you wee cunt."

"Fir fuck's sake, Sam. There is no need for that," Norman said, and helped Jonty back to his feet. The blood was coming from his nose and lip and he was still a bit dazed as Norman sat him down onto a seat. I went into the toilet and brought some toilet paper out and handed it to Jonty, who snatched it from me and said, "This is your fault, ball bag, and I won't forget it."

As Jonty wiped the blood away, I thought to myself, *It was fuck all to do with me. How the fuck do I always get dragged into these things?* So I went to the bar and lifted a cloth and put some ice in it.

"Here Jonty, this will take the swelling out, and it's not my fault. I'm only doing what Sam asks so don't be blaming me."

"Aye Jonny, aye. Just get away from me."

I walked over to Billy.

"I'm shooting on home, Billy, if you don't mind. It's been a long night."

"Aye Jonny, good idea. Tempers are raised, you'd be better getting off side."

So off I went. I was just about to walk out the door when Big Sam shouted after me, "6pm, Jonny! Make sure you're here."

I turned and said, "I'll be here, don't worry."

And out the door I went. To be honest I couldn't wait to get to the safety of my car and get home.

Thursday came round too quickly. I went down to the club for 6pm as Sam requested and when I got down Billy had already opened up. I walked in, not knowing what to expect, but was greeted by the sight of Jason and Paul, and behind them, sitting at the table, was Sam and four other men. I looked over but no sign of Jonty. I asked Jason and Paul where he was and they replied, "He won't be here. He has got a broken jaw and is just getting over surgery so you are the third man tonight. So you better be up for it."

"What? What do you mean I'm the third man? What the fuck is going on? Billy, do you know about this?" I said, looking over to where Billy was standing.

Billy looked over and he was grey-looking. He looked like a rabbit in the headlights. He replied to me, "Yes son, Sam has requested that you are the driver so you need to sit down and get your orders."

I was in total shock. What was I going to do? I was going to part of killing a man. I really didn't want to do this but had no choice, 'cause if I refused I would probably end up in hospital. I walked over to the table and said to Sam, "Sam, you need to speak with me?"

"Yes Jonny, sit down. Tonight, it is very important that it runs like clockwork. Your job is just to get the boys home."

He handed me what looked like a handheld radio.

"This is a police scanner. When you have the boys in place then you park the car just past the entrance to Belfast Castle Country Park, turn the scanner on, and listen to what the police are talking about. If there is any mention about Belfast Castle use this phone," Sam handed me a mobile phone, "and phone Paul and tell him to abort. He will then walk down and meet you, where you will drive down the road, where you will pick Jason up and return here. If all goes to plan the job will be done and yous meet me back here for 7.30. Do you understand Jonny?"

"Yes Sam, I do. When do we leave?"

Sam looked at this watch.

"It's now 6.25, we go in five minutes so get yourself together. Paul and Jason already have been prepped – they know what to do."

I looked at Billy who just shrugged his shoulders and put his head down. This was going to happen and there was no way of getting out of it. I walked over to Jason and Paul.

"Yous ready to go?"

"Yep, ready when you are, Jonny, so don't fuck it up."

We walked outside where an aul Ford Escort was waiting, and a guy got out of it. He walked over to me.

"Just watch the brakes on that motor, son. They aren't the best but it runs alright. She is half full of petrol, so good luck." He handed me the keys.

"Open the boot, Jonny," Jason said.

I walked over and put the keys in the lock and popped the boot open. Inside was a couple of aul coats and a spare wheel. Jason walked over and put a bag in and I closed the boot again.

We all got in the car and off we went. I was shitting myself. The thought of going to kill someone was making me feel sick, but I knew I had to do it.

It took me about twenty minutes to get to the first drop-off point opposite a taxi depo on the Antrim road, where Jason got out. He said to me.

"Good luck, Jonny, and fir fuck's sake stop panicking. It's not like you are pulling the trigger."

He slammed the door shut and off we went up to the country park, where I pulled in and Paul got out. He stooped down and said to me, "You will need to open the boot, Jonny. I need the bag."

"Oh, right Paul."

I turned the engine off and got out, where I opened the boot and Paul got the bag. I closed the boot and got back into the car and started it up. I turned the car and drove back out onto the Antrim road where I parked about twenty feet from the entrance. My nerves were wrecked. I lifted the police scanner and turned it on; I heard a man talking about a traffic accident on the Crumlin road, so I knew I was on the right channel to listen to the police.

It felt like an eternity, sitting, waiting, and listening. I kept looking at my watch – 7 o'clock, then five past, then ten past. Nothing was happening, then all of a sudden a taxi went past me and turned into the park.

"Fuck, this is it. Fuck, this is it," I said as I wound

my window down. I poked my head out and heard shots being fired. One, two, three, four, five, six shots fired in total. Then I saw Paul run down to the car, where he jumped into the back seat. As I started the car he shouted, "Fir fuck's sake! Go, go, go, go!"

I sped off down the Antrim road where Jason was waiting. I pulled over and he got in. He said to Paul, "Did you get him? Did you kill the I.R.A. bastard?"

"Yes, I got him. Four in the chest and two in the head. There is fuck all left of his face; he's a dead man alright."

As we drove down the Antrim road a police car with its lights and horn on came flying up past us, closely followed by an ambulance. We pulled down onto Carlisle Circus roundabout and turned up the Crumlin road, where we drove straight into a police road block. I braked and said, "Fuck, we are caught. We are caught."

Paul said, "Calm down Jonny, calm down. It's just a routine check. Just be calm and don't panic."

As I wound down my window; the policeman looked in.

"Where are you going, lads?"

I replied, "Just back up home, mister." My heart was thumping.

"And where is home, son?"

"Shankill, mister." I couldn't say any more than two words. I was an absolute wreck.

He looked into the car at Jason and Paul. "Just out a wee run in the motor then?"

"Aye, just a wee run," Paul replied.

Just at that, I heard the policeman's radio go.

"Be on the lookout for a blue Escort, it's been involved in a shooting. Report back if you see it, but don't stop it as the occupants will be carrying."

The policeman turned his radio off and said to me, "You better get this car off the road, son, before anyone else sees it. Now go on, get away up the road."

He stood back and waved us on. As I drove up the Crumlin road I turned to Jason and said, "What the fuck, Jason? He knew it was us. Why did he let us go?"

"Well Big Sam said we were going to have a clear run home, so that must have been it."

I drove the car back to the club where Sam and other men were waiting for us. As soon as we walked into the club, Sam stood up.

"Well? Was it a success, Paul?" he asked.

"Yes Sam, mission accomplished."

They all cheered in the bar like it was a celebration, slapping the three of us on the back like we were heroes. I just kept thinking, *A man has just lost his life and I was part of it.* I couldn't even lift my head to look at Billy. He walked over to me.

"Jonny, are you ok son?"

"Not really, Billy. I'm sick to my stomach."

"You will be ok, son. There was nothing you could of done. If you had of refused it would have been your mum identifying your body, so just remember that."

"I know, Billy. It will be the last. I'm never doing anything like that again. We nearly got caught by the peelers as well but they let us go."

"I know, Jonny. We were listening to the police scanner. We heard the message come through but Big Sam was already told that yous had a free passage home."

"What's going to happen now, Billy?"

Just at that, Sam spoke up.

"Jonny, have you the keys of the motor?"

I reached into my pocket and lifted them out.

"Yes Sam, here they are."

I handed them to him and he turned round to one of the men.

"Here, you know what to do."

He handed him the keys; the man stood up and said, "I will be back shortly, lads. Keep a pint for me," and off he went.

I said to Billy, "Where is he going, Billy?"

"To burn the motor, son, so there is no evidence."

"Oh right, then I can't be connected to the motor then?"

"Yes, son. The sooner that motor is burnt the better."

About an hour later the man returned. He walked straight over to Sam.

"That's it done, gaffer. No evidence left."

"Spot on, Jim. Well done. Billy, get a round of

drinks in for the lads, we are celebrating tonight."

I sat there for about another hour over a pint, which every time I took a drink of, I felt sick. The rest of them were celebrating like it was the 12th of July. I couldn't wait to get out of there and get home. Billy told me to take the next week off. I think he knew how I felt about what had happened and knew I needed a break.

CHAPTER 26

Time To Think

My week off, and I spent most of the time getting the house finished off. My mum was well made up; our wee house was lovely. I have never seen so many bloody mirrors in my life – on the wall, the TV cabinet was mirrored, the set of tables, again, mirrored, and even the bloody lamp that sat on the table was mirrored. I swear when the sun shined in through our front window the place lit up like Blackpool Illuminations. You couldn't see the TV properly. I needed a pair of sunglasses but my mum was chuffed and that's all that mattered.

I spent a couple of days with Karen but she was working, so it was only a couple. We took a race to Newcastle and had a go on the dodgems, which was quite competitive. I think I got whiplash from the many times she side-swiped me, but it was a good laugh. We drove to Tullymore Forest, where we went for a walk. When the rain came on we sat in one of the wee huts that were on the route. As we sat there we began to chat.

"Listen Karen, we have been going out for a while now and I really love being with you. Days like today I could spend the rest of my days doing."

"I know, Jonny. I feel the same. I love being with you too. Even when I'm not with you I'm thinking about you. I have had a few boyfriends but never felt like this. Oh my god, I don't believe I'm even saying this. I'm embarrassed." She put her head in her hands; I put my arm round her.

"Don't be embarrassed, I feel the same way. I count the hours until I'm with you again. I haven't had many girlfriends but I know I just want you."

"Seriously, Jonny? A good looker like you? I thought you would have been beating the girls back."

I laughed. "Are your eyes painted on? You must be taking the hand?"

"No, Jonny. I think you're lovely."

"Karen, I think you're a stunner. A real head turner."

We leant in and kissed. I had kissed Karen lots of times but this was different. I had fallen in love with her and I think at that moment she had with me. We must have kissed for a good ten minutes until I felt Karen's hand rub up the inside of my leg. Higher she went, higher. Holy fuck, I was as horny as anything, then I heard a voice.

"Here boy, come on away and stop annoying them two lovebirds."

We immediately stopped kissing. I opened my eyes and there was a bloody big dog with his nose stuck near my balls.

"Fuck me," I said, and shooed the dog away.

"Sorry about that mate," the man said.

I burst out laughing.

Karen said to me, "What's so funny Jonny?"

"Nothing Karen, that dog just scared the crap out of me. I thought it was your hand but the dog had other ideas."

We both sat there laughing in the rain. It was definitely something I would remember all my days.

After we stopped laughing I lifted a pen knife out of my pocket and carved both our names into the side of the hut, and drew a heart round them. As I stood there finishing it off I turned to Karen.

"Have you ever thought of getting married?"

I turned back straight away. I could feel my face burn.

"Yeah Jonny, I have. Why? Are you asking?"

"Maybe. I love you, Karen, and could spend the rest of my life with you." I turned to face her. "Will you marry me, Karen?"

Karen stood up. She took one step over to me and held both my hands. She looked into my eyes.

"Yes, Jonny Andrews. I would be proud to be called your wife."

"Oh my god, Karen. We are really going to do this."

I kissed her again and held her really tight. The rain got heavier; I could hear it bounce off the roof of the wooden hut, and I stood there, the proudest man alive. I was going to treat Karen like a queen. I loved her with all my heart and I knew she loved me too.

We made a dash to get back to the car but the big steep hill we had to run up was too much for us both so we walked, and by the time we got back to the car we were soaked to the skin, but it didn't matter, the two of us just laughed about it. I got a blanket that I had in the boot of the car and gave it to Karen. I swear she was a magician; she was able to take her clothes off while sitting in the car with the blanket round her. Me, I just started the car to get the heating on. I was bloody freezing.

"Typical Nor'n Iron weather, isn't it Karen?"

"Aye Jonny, you couldn't plan anything."

As I drove the car back through Newcastle, I pulled up outside a clothes shop and said to Karen, "What size of jeans are you and what size of top?"

She looked at me. "You never ask a lady her clothes size, Jonny."

"I will remember that, but what size are you?"

She laughed. "Cheeky bugger, I'm a size ten. Why?"

"I can't take you home naked for Christ's sake. Your da would hit me a thump."

"Don't be daft. My da likes you better than me, I'm sick listening to him about you."

"I want to buy you jeans and a top so, you mind the car and I will be back in a minute."

I got out of the car and went into the shop where I was greeted by a girl about the same age as Karen and about the same size. She said to me, "Can I help you, sir?"

I looked round then looked back.

"Me?" I pointed to myself.

"Yes sir, I don't see anyone else here," she replied.

"I've never been called sir before, just call me Jonny."

"Ok Jonny. Can I help you?"

"Yes, I'm looking for a pair of jeans and a top for my girlfriend. She is a size ten if that helps."

"That's the size I am, so yes, I can help you. These over here are very popular."

She walked over to a rack of jeans and pulled out a pair.

"I have a pair of these, so what do you think?"

They were blue with a few rips in the legs. I said to the girl, "Yeah, they are nice, but are them ones not damaged?"

She laughed. "No, Jonny, that's the style."

I laughed as well. "Well if that's the style then I will take them. What about a wee top to match?"

"These ones over here are nice."

As she lifted one of them off the rail to show me, I just thought, *Must get that in white, especially with Karen not wearing a bra. Pure genius.*

"Yep, I will take one of them in white, size ten, if you have it?"

The girl lifted the top out and said, "Is that all you need?"

"Yea that's me sorted, thanks."

And we walked to the till to pay.

When I returned to the car and gave Karen her clothes, again, she was like a magician under that blanket. She got the clothes on and yep, good choice with the white top.

"Karen, you look cold, do you want to turn the heating up?"

She looked down and noticed that her nipples were quite noticeable through her top; she leant over and hit me with a dig on the leg.

"See you Jonny, you miss nothing."

And she folded her arms across her chest and laughed. I laughed as well and we started the drive home.

When I pulled up outside Karen's house I gave her a kiss and said, "See you Saturday. I will pick you up about one. We are going into town to get a ring."

She leant across, threw her arms round me and said, "Yes Jonny. I love you, you know."

"Yeah Karen, I do, and I love you too," I replied.

Karen got out of the car and I drove off. I turned the radio on – Cool FM was on and slow songs were playing. Peter Cetera, The Glory of Love was playing and I thought it was really good. A song you could dance the first dance of your wedding to.

On Saturday I picked Karen up and we went into town. We walked round a couple of jewellers and Karen picked a lovely diamond ring with a blue stone in it out of H. Samuels. Not too bad either – 300 quid, so I decided to take her down to City Hall and on the steps I got down on one knee and asked her to marry me. Her face was red but she replied yes and when I stood up I hadn't noticed a crowd of people had gathered behind me. They all cheered as I hugged Karen and gave her a kiss. Pure scundered, we were, but it was worth it and we walked down to one of the wee local bars for lunch and a celebratory drink.

When we got back to Karen's mum and dad's house we walked in and I said to her dad, "Alan, can I have a word please?"

"Yes son, what is it?" he replied.

"I mean in private."

"Of course, son. Come on, we will go out to the garden."

We walked out to their back garden and I said, "Alan, me and Karen have been going out for a while now and I'm not ashamed to say it, I love her and I would like to marry her if you have no objections."

He stood there for what was about two lifetimes and then replied, "If you ever hurt my wee girl I will take you back up the Shankill and have you done in."

The blood drained from me. "I would never hurt her, Alan. I love her."

"I know, son. I'm only messing with you." And he threw his arms round me. "Welcome to the family, son. I would be proud to call you my son-in-law."

Just at that, Karen and her mum came out and Karen's face said it all. She was beaming and her mum was smiling as well. She showed her dad the ring and he gave her a big hug.

That night Karen's mum and dad took us out to the Park Avenue Hotel for a meal and few drinks. It was absolutely brilliant; anyone that Alan knew, he introduced me to them as his future son-in-law. It was a real nice feeling. Even her wee sister got on well with me – it was perfect.

I stayed over at Karen's house that night. On the settee, I may add. Sandra and Alan were very strict like that – no sex before marriage. If only they knew what we got up to in the back of my motor.

The next morning over breakfast Sandra asked us, "Well have yous thought about a date for the big day?"

Me and Karen looked at each other and she replied, "No Mum, we haven't, but we want to get a house before we get married so we are going to start saving."

I piped up. "We were thinking maybe two years to give us time to do it right."

Alan said, "Yous are probably right, it takes a lot of money to get married these days."

If only Alan and Sandra knew I was sitting on about twenty-five grand. We could have got married next week if we wanted, but again, I couldn't tell anyone about the money – not even Karen.

I started back at work on the Monday and to be honest things had changed. As the week went on the atmosphere in the club was different. I didn't know what it was but maybe with Big Sam now running the road and with his mentality, everyone was walking on egg shells. Big Sam was a nasty piece of work, even Billy didn't like him and he never said a bad word about anyone. But my opinion was that if you crossed him you were signing your own death warrant, so every time there was a meeting I did my best to let Billy stay on 'cause I knew who would be attending, and I knew Jonty still held a grudge with me after Sam had broken his jaw. So I knew at some stage I would have to stand up to him, and I really didn't want it to come to that 'cause I was on a beaten docket. I did my best to avoid him at every opportunity.

*

A week or so had passed and on the Shankill, there was a fallout between the U.V.F. and Sam's crew, the U.F.F. Two murders had taken place – one from each side. A meeting was to take place and I was to stay on to serve drinks and to lock up.

10.30pm one Thursday in November, 1996.

I started my normal shift, 6pm till whatever. I did my usual things – light the fire, bottle up, and wipe down the tables and bar. The doors opened at 7pm and the darts were on, so an easy enough night. They were finished about 10 but at 9.30 Sam and his crew came in and sat in the corner. I noticed that only Paul was with them so I was relieved and just kept serving drinks to whoever needed them. Billy said to me he needed to leave early as his wife had started a new job and was on the nightshift, so he needed to be home for eleven. I didn't mind as we weren't busy, so he left shortly after ten, just as the darts had finished. I started lifting glasses and it was when I got over to Sam's table, he said to me, "Can you stay on tonight, Jonny? We have a bit of business to attend to."

I didn't like his tone. The last time I heard him speak like that I was ordered to be part of a murder, so it worried me a bit, but I could only give him one reply.

"Yes Sam, that's not a problem."

I just kept going on with sorting the bar out, and when the last punter had left Sam walked out and pulled the shutter down, and came in. He had just said to Paul, "Right son, get it ready. They will be hear shortly."

Paul got up and started lifting chairs and tables from the middle of the floor. He cleared three tables and twelve chairs. I was confused by what was going on but really worried as well. It was when he went into the back store and came out with a roll of plastic and rolled it into the area he had just cleared that I started really getting scared. I thought to myself, *What the hell's going on?* But when he put a single chair in the middle of the plastic and asked me to turn all the lights off, just leaving the dart board lights on, that I knew something was going down. But there was nowhere for me to go. If I made a bolt for it I would be a dead man, so I went behind the bar and looked round to see if there was anything I could use to defend myself, but when I looked at who was in the room, I knew even if I had a gun they would still get me, so I stood there trying to blend into the background and not be noticed.

After serving them drinks for about an hour they were starting to get impatient. Big Sam was walking round the floor like a caged lion.

"Where the fuck are they? They should have been here," he said in anger.

The only ones I could think of that should have been there were Jonty and Jason, and I didn't like the look of what was going to happen if they turned up. The longer the night went on, the more and more paranoid I got. I heard the shutter go up and my heart skipped a beat. In fact, it was beating a mile a minute. I was shitting myself, to be honest.

Jonty and Jason came in, pulling a man between them with a cloth bag over his head. They pulled him over to where the chair was and sat him down.

"About fucking time," Sam said. "I was beginning to think you two had got fucking lost."

"No Sam, just took a bit of time to find him, but we are here now," Jonty replied.

I stood there in Heather Street Social Club, sort of relieved as I thought the chair was for me, but scared as fuck at the thought of what they were going to do to this man.

Sam lifted another chair and sat in front of the man, who was sitting with his head slumped. He lifted his chin and said to him, "You're one of the Kellys, aren't you?"

The man nodded.

Sam said, "What's wrong? Cat got your tongue?"

"I'm not telling you nothing, you bastards."

Sam hit him a punch in the face and his head rocked back.

"That's all the fun of it, you Fenian bastard. I would prefer you didn't tell me anything 'cause you're going to be here a while and I'm going to enjoy watching you suffer."

The blood ran cold in my body. Again, I was

caught up in another situation I really didn't want to be involved in.

"Jonty, go and get the tools," Sam said as he walked over to the bar. "Jonny, put some music on please. Something tasteful."

I was numb. I reached down behind the bar and turned the amp on and CD player. I hoked for a CD to put on and the first one I came to was bloody Kenny Rogers, so I put it on and pressed play. The Gambler started playing and it reminded me of my da, but one of the men called over, "Jonny, put number six on. I like that one."

I reached down and pressed forward on the CD player to number six, and it started playing. I recognised it straight away after years of listening to it on my da's drunken nights in the house – Coward of the County.

Sam walked over just as Jonty came back in with a heavy-looking bag, and took the cloth bag off the man's head.

*

I stood there in shock. It was Gerrerd they had lifted, and it looked like he was going to be executed. I shouted, "I know him! He's not who you think he is!"

I ran from behind the bar over to where Gerrerd was sitting. He lifted his head and just smiled. He had blood running from his nose and round his eyes was swollen as well. I leant down to his level. "Gerrerd, it's me, Jonny. You will be ok, I will get this stopped."

Just at that, I got punched in the back of the head and fell into Gerrerd. We both fell to the floor in a heap. I struggled to get to my feet, where Jonty was standing.

"I fucking knew it Sam. He's the one we have been looking for. He's the one feeding our information to the I.R.A."

He punched me again. This time I didn't go down but I hit back and got stuck into Jonty. Years of putting up with his bulling just came to a boil in that instant, but I only got a couple of digs in when I was pulled off him. I was screaming at him by this stage.

"I will kill you, you wee fucker!"

But another punch from behind and I was out cold.

When I came round I was sitting beside Gerrerd, strapped to a chair. Sam was standing in front of us just waiting. I looked up.

"Sam, what the fuck is going on?" I said.

"Jonny, someone from in this room has been giving information to the I.R.A. That is how they have been able to target our crew, and it is quite evident it's you."

"No Sam! No way. I would never do that. You have got it wrong."

"Well Jonny, someone has to pay and it's you."

And at that, he said to Jonty, "Get a table over, son, and get the tools out."

Jonty walked over with a real smirk on his face when he looked at me, and lifted a table over beside where Sam was standing. He then lifted the bag over, which he brought in from the car, and opened it. He lifted out a hammer, a box of nails, and a pair of pliers. There were a few other items but I couldn't really see.

I turned my head to look at Gerrerd and he was a mess; he looked at me and I could see in his eyes he was petrified. I think we both knew what was coming.

Sam said to Jonty, "Right, get started."

Jonty lifted the hammer and walked over to where we were sitting. He said to Gerrerd, "Right, you have one chance and one chance only to answer Sam's questions, and if you don't I am going to make you answer. Do you understand?"

Gerrerd lifted his head and spat at Jonty. *Big mistake*, I thought.

Jonty swung the hammer and it came down on Gerrerd's kneecap. I could hear his kneecap shatter and Gerrerd squealed; he was in agony.

Jonty said again, "No chances now. If you want more, keep it up, you Fenian bastard."

Sam put his hand on Jonty's shoulder. "Give me a minute, Jonty."

Jonty looked at me and smiled. He turned his back as Sam sat down on a chair opposite us.

"We can do this the easy way or my way, it's up to you, son. Now let's start with your name."

"Gerrerd Kelly," Gerrerd answered.

"Now that's not too hard, is it?"

"No," Gerrerd replied.

"Now tell me this. What is your relationship to Sean Kelly?"

"Nothing, we aren't related."

Sam looked round at Jonty, who immediately swung his hammer and hit Gerrerd on the shoulder and broke his collarbone. Gerrerd cried with pain.

"I swear, I am nothing to do with Sean. Nothing!"

"You see, son. We know different. Your da and his da are brothers, which makes you cousins, and to be honest anybody related to that I.R.A. bastard should be dead."

"No mister, you have got it wrong. I know him, yes, but that's all and I am not like him. I play football and stay away from all that."

"After tonight, son, your football career is over. Now it's about you wanting to survive and how far you will go to make sure we don't kill you here and now."

I spoke up. The nerves in my voice were quiet apparent when I started speaking.

"Sam, I told you, I know him. I met him a few years back and we played for the Milk Cup team. He is right when he tells you he plays football; he is a Cliftonville player. He isn't in the I.R.A. He comes form a good family and isn't mixed up in anything."

I had just finished speaking when Jonty lashed out at me; he hit me with the hammer on my ribcage and the pain was horrific. I fell to the floor, wincing in pain. I heard him say, "Fuck up, Fenian lover. You're here to watch, not talk."

He grabbed me by the hair and pulled me and the chair back up.

I sat there, in pain and really frightened, but that was when Sam said, "Right Gerrerd, you are going to work for us now. I want the names and addresses of any known I.R.A. who live in Ardoyne, and if you don't help us out then I will let Jonty have his fun."

Gerrerd lifted his blood soaked head and just smiled. I don't know why he did that. Probably he knew no matter what he did he was a dead man, and there was no escaping what was about to take place.

Jonty walked over to the fire and lifted the poker. He started poking the fire and left the poker in it as he lifted the bucket of coal and threw some on. He then walked back over to Sam and said, "Well Sam, what's it to be?"

Sam looked at me and then at Gerrerd, whose head was just rocking back and forward slightly.

"Well Gerrerd, what's it to be?"

Gerrerd replied, "Fuck you, do your worst."

Oh my god. I couldn't believe he just said that. I looked on in horror as Jonty just laughed and said, "Right answer, dick head."

He turned to the table and lifted the nails; they were about four inches long. He got to his knees and placed one of the nails on the centre of Gerrerd's foot. He hit it with the hammer again and again until Gerrerd's foot was nailed to the floor. The squeals from Gerrerd where deafening, until he passed out.

Jonty lifted a small bottle form the table and opened its lid. He pulled back Gerrerd's head and held it under his nose. About ten seconds passed and Gerrerd started coughing. The tears were freely running down his cheeks as he continued to cough.

Jonty then said, "Back with the living again, Taig."

He lifted another nail and proceeded to nail Gerrerd's other foot to the floor. The cries from Gerrerd really upset me and I could feel tears run down my cheeks, but I knew I couldn't say a word.

Sam then said, "Do you understand, Gerrerd, that we will get the information no matter what? If it's not you it will be the next one, so you might as well do the decent thing and save someone else's life, and we will stop."

Again Gerrerd lifted his head. He spat a mouthful of blood at Sam and said, "I'm not telling you fuck all."

Sam hit him with such a punch to the head I swear I think he broke his neck, as Gerrerd's head flew straight back again. Jonty grabbed Gerrerd by the hair and put that bottle under his nose to bring him round. Gerrerd coughed and opened his eyes but only barely; he was in a real state and his head was slumped forward with blood running from him in numerous places. I felt helpless but fearful that Jonty would turn on me.

Sam then said, "Well if you're not going to talk to me then you won't talk again."

Jonty walked over to the now blazing fire and lifted the glowing poker out. He walked back over to Gerrerd and lifted his head. He said, "Open your mouth, you fucker, and you're going to bite down on this."

Gerrerd was barely conscious but he opened his mouth and Jonty placed the red hot poker in.

I turned my head away quickly but Sam grabbed it and made me watch. The smoke coming from

Gerrerd's face was terrible and the smell of burning was making me gag. In fact, I was sick all over myself and that bastard Jonty just stood there laughing as Gerrerd's mouth was melting and bits of skin fell onto his lap.

Sam said, "Right, that's enough Jonty. Take it out."

As Jonty took the poker out of Gerrerd's mouth some teeth came along with it and he just threw Gerrerd to the floor. He said, "I'm finished with this one. What about Jonny, Sam? Will I give him a rearranged face as well?"

As he pointed the poker towards me, Sam said, "No, Jonty. I believe him when he said he only knew him through football so you won't touch him."

"Fuck's sake, Sam. Just a wee bit?" Jonty asked.

"I told you before, my decision is final. Now put the poker away and let's get these two out of here and get the place clean."

Gerrerd was lying in a heap on the floor. I didn't know if he was alive or dead but it was when Jonty got the hammer and pulled the nails out of his feet that I knew he was still alive, 'cause he winced in pain and just curled up in a ball, holding his head.

I was in a mess myself but nowhere near the pain Gerrerd was in.

Two men lifted Gerrerd off the floor and trailed him outside. I was pulled outside as well and put into the back of a car. Gerrerd was shoved into the boot and Jonty, Paul, and Jason got into the car as well. Sam leant into the car and said to Jonty, "You know what to do but don't touch Jonny. Leave him at the top of the road."

"Ok Sam, we will be back soon."

As we drove up the Shankill and up onto the Woodvale, I said to Jason, "Where am I getting out?"

He turned to me and said, "You're not."

I tried to open the door to jump out but it was locked and Jason started punching me until I fell to the floor of the car, where he started stamping on me. I just lay there taking it. I couldn't do anything else – I was trapped.

We turned a few times but I hadn't got a clue where we were when the car stopped. I just knew it was dark and the dimly lit street could have been anywhere.

As I was being pulled from the car, so was Gerrerd, and we were trailed up an entry where we lay side by side. I heard Jason say to Jonty, "Sam isn't going to be too happy."

Jonty replied, "Fuck Sam, he is getting soft in his old age."

And *BANG* the pain in my leg. Jonty had just kneecapped me.

"Fenian lover," he said.

And *BANG*, my other knee done. I curled up in pain and then I heard Jonty say, "I.R.A. bastard."

I opened my eyes and looked at Gerrerd just as Jonty pulled the trigger. For one split moment we were free, free from pain, but *BANG*, and Gerrerd's head shot forward and the fear in his eyes was gone.

Car doors slammed with the screech of tyres, and

everything went silent. It started raining and I was lying there soaked in blood, but felt no pain. I could hear my heartbeat and it was getting slower and slower. I could hear sirens in the distance and I prayed they were for me…

Printed in Great Britain
by Amazon